DARK
SIDE
OF
AMERICA

DARK
SIDE
OF
AMERICA

RICHARD
GREGORY
BRITNER III

Pleasant W rd
A Division of WINEPRESS PUBLISHING

ISBN 1-4141-0479-0
Library of Congress Catalog Card Number: 2005903956

TABLE OF CONTENTS

FOREWORD

The Spirit clearly says that in later times some will
abandon the faith and follow decieving spirits and
things taught by demons. Such teachings come through
hypocritical liars, whose consciences have been seared
as with a hot iron.

—1 Timothy 4:1-2

This story actually begains in a different time, a different era. At this time there is a tyrant abroad. A tyrant
who was the offspring of tyrants. It was said that
the sun never set on the British Empire. The lands that fell
under the realm of this tyrant extended from India, Africa,
Australia, and the colonies of America. Truly, the sun never
did set on this empire.

As it is with an empire of this size, it needed large
numbers of soldiers to maintain its grip on these foreign
soils. Such a massive army required pay for its soldiers and
numerous supplies. This, of course, meant taxation.

Like so many others before him, this tyrant cared little for those subjects on foreign soil. He placed exorbitant taxes on these people to support those very soldiers that policed their country. In one of these lands, the people sent representatives to the tyrant, petitioning for fairer laws and more reasonable taxation. But this tyrant, King George III, responded with only harsher laws and additional taxes.

It became apparent to the people of this land that no relief from burdensome taxes would be forthcoming. Men of noble character, more noble than the nobility who ruled them, rose up and expressed ideas of freedom and self-rule. They talked about breaking their ties with the present abusive and oppresive government, which had outlived its usefulness, and establishing a new government that aspired to adopt more godly principles. They knew that for a nation to be free and democratic, God and His teachings would have to be prevalent.

Documents were written, treaties were signed, and a war was fought. The United States became a free nation, and the men who led the way set up a new government—a government that was to be for the people, run by the people. Certain safeguards were put in place to ensure that this new nation would never again know the burdensome, slave-like state of tyranny.

But as time passed, the people begain to forget the oppressive nature of rule under a tyrant. As the leaders, elected by the people, began to taste power, these protections that the founders of America set in place began to slip away. States gradually gave up their sovereign status and became more dependent on the central government for aid. The federal government slowly increased its own authority. Little by little the people unwittingly yielded their rights and freedoms.

The nation that the founders had birthed underwent a transformation. A new type of tyranny came alive. Blinded by pseudo-patriotic propaganda, the people did not see this new tyrant raise his ugly head. They scarcely felt the new tyrant tightening his grip. The burden of taxes increased. Laws also increased, reaching a stifling number. These laws were not designed to protect the innocent but to control the thoughts of men and manipulate their actions. A new slave state began to rise, separating those in power—the new nobility—from the new peasantry.

Not all the people were blind to this deceitful takeover. Understanding the principles upon which this nation was founded, many Christians spoke out and resisted this tyranny.

To combat this resistance there was only one thing for this new tyranny to do. Those in power would have to eliminate Christians, so their clandestine, hate-filled campaign began. They could not lose. The deck was stacked in their favor. Too few brave people remained in this nation to oppose them. Too few realized the truth—yet some still did.

ACKNOWLEDGMENTS

I never would have accomplished the writing of this book by myself. First I would like to thank God and the Holy Spirit without whose inspiration I could not have done anything. My wife Stacy's typing skills and ability to read my writing were paramount to the completion of this book. She patiently proofread the material throughout the writing process.

Several friends also provided assistance. Jeff Wald tried to recover all of my lost work when my floppy disk—the only place I had saved my manuscript—malfunctioned. Stacy retyped what had been lost. Roxanne Becerra looked up information for me on the Internet.

The professionals at the Focus on the Family Institute assisted me with a few facts I could not find for myself. Dr. Dobson, you should be proud of your team. Finally, I would like to thank all of the authors and publishers of the books and articles that I used as references. You provide a great service in helping to keep people informed.

CHAPTER 1

REFLECTIONS

Thomas Archippus stepped onto the porch of his rental and drank in a deep breath of the cool, crisp, early morning air. It was too early—way too early—for a Saturday for Thomas's liking. The clock had just turned to a quarter after six. Thomas normally wouldn't think of getting out of bed until eight at the earliest.

Despite the sunny and mostly clear skies, Thomas could see his breath on this late April day. He debated for a second or two about going back in the house for a light jacket. He had only a short walk ahead of him. It was expected to reach sixty-two degrees today, so he opted to endure the cold for now. As he started for the campus, the sun was just above the eastern range. The few clouds in the east hung in pastel shades of red and orange against the light blue canopy.

Helena, Montana sat nested in a large valley surrounded by mountains on all four sides. Being from Lakewood, Colorado, Thomas did not consider these mountains as majestic as the ones back home. Some he would call only foothills, but they were mountains, and that made a world of difference to him. He liked mountains!

He thought about the events that led to his being up at the crack of dawn. A few days earlier Sam Stein, with whom he rented a house on Leslie Avenue, Paul Archor, John Watchman, and he were driving to Stinky Burgers for a bite to eat and a game of pool. In response to a newscast he had heard on the radio, Thomas mentioned that John Kerry sounded like a possible candidate for president. Sam and Paul cringed and said, "Yuk! Ugh!"

John, who was driving, shook his head and said, "Sam, it looks like academia is seducing your roomy to the dark side."

"Yeah, if we don't do something quick, he might turn out to be a liberal."

"Jawohl!" chimed in Paul.

"Shall we save his life?" Sam asked John.

"Of course! What are friends for? Tom, will you meet me at the school library Saturday morning for a... well, for a game? Kind of a game."

"What kind of a game?"

Suspicion crept into Thomas's mind. These three tended to be pranksters, and he was not so sure if they were pulling his leg or not.

John paused for a second then said, "It's kind of a murder mystery game, like those mysteries that a dinner playhouse might put on. But this is about a genocide that took place over seventy years ago, and the killer is still on the loose. We believe he or she will try to commit genocide again, but this time it will be much more devastating. Will you see if you have what it takes to solve the case?"

"A real genocide seventy years old. Is this something the cops have solved or what?" Thomas asked, suspicious of John's intent. He was still leery about being suckered into a gag.

John shook his head. "No, the cops wouldn't even acknowledge that it occurred. How about it, will you meet me on Saturday?"

"What kind of mass killing won't the cops acknowledge?" Thomas asked.

"Meet me on Saturday and you'll find out," John insisted.

"Well, what…" Thomas started, but John cut him off.

"Meet me on Saturday and you'll get an answer to all your questions."

"Go for it!" Paul added. "I did it and it was an eye-opener."

Thomas looked to Sam.

"I helped John find the information, so I definitely say go," Sam encouraged him.

Maybe this is not a gag, Thomas thought.

"Are you going to be there?" he asked Sam.

"No, I work in the morning," Sam replied.

Thomas looked to John as he pulled into the parking lot of Stinky Burgers. "What time do you want me to be at the library?"

"Six-thirty."

"Six-thirty! In the morning?" Now he knew John had to be joking.

"Yeah, this is going to take a few hours, and the gang is planning to eat dinner and watch *Hidalgo* at the Circus," John said, referring to the local theater.

"Oh, yeah! But the library doesn't even open until eight," Thomas replied.

"You forget that I work in the library. I can arrange it so we can get in there a little early."

"Yeah! But six-thirty?" Thomas complained.

15

Sam said, "Cowboy up, Tom." Mountain lingo for "get tough." He would receive no sympathy with this crowd.

Thomas had reached the crosswalk at Benton Avenue that led from the neighborhood to the campus. Although very little traffic passed through here on a Saturday morning, out of habit Thomas looked both ways before crossing. Despite the signs posted in both directions to stop for pedestrians, you had a 50 percent chance of a driver speeding up when a person entered the crosswalk.

No cars, no problem. This sidewalk led pretty much to the center of the campus. Carroll College was a mixture of old and new. A college operated by the Catholic diocese, it was originally constructed in 1909 of reddish-brown, rough cut stone with a neo-Gothic style that gave the school character and charm. The newer class buildings were modern versions of the old and esthetically pleasing in their own right.

On the way to the library Thomas passed the statue that was the centerpiece of the campus. Like so many things that one sees routinely, Thomas didn't even notice it. He passed by as if the statue were invisible. On he continued to the library.

Corette Library sat at the top of a fairly steep hill. The now grassy hill sloped downward on the north to the practice field of Carroll College's Saints football team. The soccer field lay more to the east. Between these fields, just a few yards farther north, sat the newly constructed football stadium. Montanans like their college football, and the Saints were the NAIA national champions that year. This hill was the favorite sledding location for the residents of Helena. During the winter months after a good snow, the hill would be covered with children and a kaleidoscope of sleds. Thomas appreciated the steepness of the hill and the extra exertion needed to climb it. He shivered and regretted leaving his jacket behind. Too late. He was almost there.

Hope they turn on the heat on weekends, he thought as he made his way up the street.

The library was just ahead. John waited for him at the foyer and opened the door as he approached. This was the first time that he had been inside Corette during non-school hours, never so early.

The library was designed on the open room concept. Although traditionally quiet, as libraries are, the normal sounds of activity still flooded the environment that comes from people conducting business—the hum of computers, the whispers, and the shuffling of books. But now, as they walked down the stairwell, each footstep reverberated off the walls as if to announce their intrusion into the prevailing silence. The vast shelving seemed to scrutinize and almost reprimand them for violating the library's cherished solitude of the early morning hours.

"Good morning!" John whispered as they descended the stairway. "It's kind of intimidating to talk out loud when it echoes like this."

"It's actually kind of creepy."

"I know we are the only ones here right now," John smiled. "Thanks for coming, Tom. I know how much you need your beauty rest."

"Yeah, looks like you could hibernate for the winter," chided Thomas.

"Ready to get started at our game?"

"What is the goal of this game?" inquired Thomas.

"An event happened about seventy years ago, a type of genocide that…"

"Type of genocide?"

DARK SIDE OF AMERICA

"You'll see. A type of a genocide that will set the stage for the killers to commit another genocide in the near future."

"Mass murder? A guy who committed murder seventy years ago would have to be in his nineties. Where is this guy gonna commit mass murder? In a geriatric ward?" Thomas asked skeptically.

"No." John grinned again. Then he got solemn. "I think it will be a lot more devastating than that. Let's get started and you'll see for yourself."

"Hey, that's what I'm here for. What are the ground rules?"

"Simple. I'll present the evidence, and you see if you can figure out the first victim and the assassin's hand. Then see if you can figure out who hired the assassin and who his next victims will be."

Thomas nodded his head.

"Sounds good. Give me the first clues."

"Not so fast," John said. "A good detective learns as much about the victims as he can before he digs into a case. It helps him know what direction he needs to go with his questioning. First we're going to have to examine a little history."

John Watchman knew something about detective work. Although he was born and raised in Butte, Montana, he came from a long line of New York City police officers. His family tree could be traced back to the prerevolutionary era, and all the men had worked in some sort of law enforcement.

Long before John was even a thought, his father, Zeke Watchman, had graduated from the New York City police academy. He and his buddies had decided to take some leave before hitting the streets with their FTOs (Field Training Officers). One of his buddies thought they should go fishing, so the group decided they would venture into the wilds of Montana and fish the Missouri.

Zeke had never fished in his life. That didn't matter. He figured he'd be drinking more beer than fishing, so he was game. As it turned out, Montana was more intoxicating for Zeke than the beer he had brought. He had never known such openness, and the scenery awed him. Angling turned out to be the biggest thrill yet. After just ten minutes he had his first hit. His friend, an experienced fisherman, helped him reel it in.

"Reel in now, give just a little slack. Now lift the rod a little, now reel in the slack."

The fish fought, and Zeke played it for ten more minutes. When he finally netted the fish, he had a twenty-two-inch rainbow trout at the end of his line. It had been more exciting than his rides on patrol during the academy.

That evening they drove into Butte for a night on the town. Zeke stopped and talked to a local police officer and found out that they were hiring. The next morning he applied for a job. Zeke finished his rookie year as a Butte Silver Bow Law Enforcement Officer.

There he met his wife Ruth and soon had the first of his three sons. Shortly after Benjamin was born, Zeke had an opportunity to advance on the force. Promotions were few and far between in this small department. Only two candidates vied for the position. Zeke had worked hard for the force, harder than any other. He knew he was the best man for the job—and he was. But the other man became the sergeant.

Zeke spiraled into a deep depression. He spent little time at home, little time with his wife, and acted as if little Benjamin wasn't even there. This continued for nearly four years. When Benjamin was three, Zeke caught him playing with a doll that the neighbor girl, who was close to Benjamin's age, had left when her mother had picked her up after she was done shopping.

"You play with a doll?" Zeke chastised his son. "You wimp! You act like a little girl anyways."

Ruth blew up and chased him out of the house with a frying pan. Out of necessity she had assumed the dominant role in the household. Even Zeke jumped when she gave orders, unless Zeke had drunk too much—which was often. Then the words flew.

It looked like Ruth was planning to leave him, the sheriff was threatening to fire him, and friends didn't want to come around. Except one—Big Jim Henson. He was definitely big—six foot four and two hundred and seventy pounds. Having the countenance of Grizzly Adams, Big Jim could intimidate anyone. But the locals knew he had the heart of a teddy bear.

Big Jim owned and ran a local tackle shop, the only place Zeke would buy his gear. They had become good friends and fishing buddies. One day Big Jim showed up at the door and told Zeke they were going fishing. For Ruth it was just a way to get Zeke out of the house, and Zeke was always easily talked into going fishing.

Big Jim didn't go to their normal fishing hole. He didn't even take Zeke to a stream. Instead he took him to his church and there shared the truth about Christ. The two talked into the night and the vast majority of the next day. Hungry and desperate, Zeke listened and learned about Christ, and a promise he had not heard of before. His heart began to soften. He accepted Christ that second day and, with Big Jim's guidance, became strong in the faith. When Zeke returned home, he openly confessed and apologized to his wife for the way he had behaved. Ruth was skeptical, but after four months of seeing her husband's transformation, she became a believer.

The family life and his work ethic returned to the level they were before his missed promotion. Zeke Junior was born shortly after that and became the apple of his eye. Three years later John was on the scene, and Zeke had been promoted to detective. He loved the work.

As John grew, he saw that Zeke, J. was definitely his dad's favorite. Zeke loved John and was a great dad, but he unmistakably favored his namesake. This actually did not bother John. The most independent of the three boys, he didn't require a lot of attention. What he received from both parents was nourishing and he was satisfied.

John sometimes felt sorry for Ben, his oldest brother. You could almost see the chasm between father and son. His father treated Ben well, but they shared no closeness. Ben was very close to his mother though.

John grew up listening to tales of real criminal cases and the various strategies his father used to solve them. It figured that he would be a criminal science major.

John had stacks of books on the table that he obtained from the bookshelves and some that he had brought from home. Thomas could see that some were indeed history books.

"The first thing I want to do," John said, "is to go over some American history. This will give you some background on the first victim some seventy years ago and an understanding of who the next victims will be. More importantly it will help in establishing motive."

"John," he said, "if this guy killed..."

"Who said it was a guy?" John interrupted.

"Then the killer was a woman?"

"Possibly not," answered John. "I want you to hear all the evidence without having any preconceived ideas as to who the killer might be. If you don't, you might even miss the killing."

Thomas nodded his understanding.

"OK, but either way the killer is going to be at least ninety. What's this guy or gal gonna do—escape from a geriatric ward and beat people with his walker? Or run them down in his wheelchair?"

Thomas laughed at his own joke and John smiled.

"Maybe. Let's find out. First let's start with some writings of the founders of our nation."

John opened the book and quickly found the page he was looking for. It was obvious to Thomas that John had been through this book a time or two before. The first author was W. V. Wells, and they would look at excerpts from his article, "Life of Samuel Adams."

"Okay, Tom. I want you to read this paragraph. Read it out loud."

Thomas took the book and began to read, "'Samuel Adams, says Hutchinson, writing to a friend, had prepared a long report, but he let Otis appear in it; and again, in another letter: the Grand Incendiary of the Province prepared a long report for a committee appointed by the town, in which, after many principles inferring independence were laid down, many resolves followed, all of them tending to sedition and mutiny, and some of them expressly denying Parliamentary authority! The report created a powerful sensation, both in America and in England where it was for some time attributed to Franklin, by whom it was republished. It is divided into the three subjects specified in the original motion. The first, in three subdivisions, considering the rights of the Colonists as men, as Christians, and as subjects, was from the pen of Samuel Adams; his original draft...'"

"Stop right there for now," John interjected. He turned some pages. "I want you to read what Patrick Henry said during his address to the Virginia convention on March 20, 1775. You don't have to read it all, just from here," John pointed to the middle of the page, "to here." His finger slid to the bottom of the page.

"You want me to read out loud?"

"Yeah. Hearing the words out loud makes it easier for most people to understand what they read."

"Yeah, it also helps the other guy know that the person actually read what you ask," Thomas replied.

John was not trying to belittle Thomas and wanted to emphasize his motive.

"True, but hearing oneself speak out loud helps a person from misinterpreting what they've read, and this is my reason for it. It's vital if you are going to understand the killer."

Thomas nodded and said, "Okay." He then read, "'In vain may we indulge the fond hope of reconciliation. There is no longer room for hope. If we wish to be free, we must fight! I repeat it, Sir, we must fight! An appeal to arms and to the God of Hosts is all that is left us: They tell me that we are weak; but shall we gather strength by irresolution? We are not weak. Three millions of people, armed in the holy cause of liberty, and in such a country, are invincible by any force which our enemy can stand against us. We shall not fight alone. A just God presides over the destinies of nations... There is no retreat, but in submission and slavery... Is life so dear, or peace so sweet as to be purchased at the price of chains and slavery? Forbid it, Almighty God! I know not what course others may take; but as for me, give me liberty or give me death.' Wow! What a speaker."

"I agree," John replied. "Read this now." John turned the pages again. "This is the writing of William Penn. He was the founder and first governor of Pennsylvania, although the territory was actually named after his father, Admiral Penn. The constitution he outlined and enacted was a model for this nation's founders when they drafted the Constitution. Here, read this paragraph."

Thomas read out loud, "'Whereas the glory of Almighty God and the good of mankind is the reason and end of government, and therefore government itself is a venerable ordinance of God, and forasmuch as it is principally devised and intended by the Proprietary and Governor and freemen of Pennsylvania and territories thereunto belonging, to make and establish such laws as shall best preserve true Christian, and civil liberty, in opposition to all unchristian, licentious, and unjust practices, whereby God may have his due, Caesar his due, and the people their due...'"

While Thomas reflected on what he read, John pulled out another book from his backpack that contained pieces of paper marking pages. John opened to the first marker.

"I want you to read some quotes. First read George Washington's."

"'It is impossible to rightly govern the world without God and the Bible.'"

John pointed at a different line and said, "Read what Thomas Jefferson asked."

"'And can the liberties of a nation be thought secure when we have removed their only firm basis, a conviction in the minds of the people that these liberties are a gift of God?'"

"Good! Go ahead and read the quotes from John Quincy Adams and John Adams."

"Okay. John Quincy Adams said, 'The highest glory of the American Revolution was this; it connected in one indissoluble bond the principles of civil government with the principles of Christianity.' John Adams said, 'Religion and virtue are the only foundations, not only of republicanism and of all free government, but of social felicity under all governments and in all the combinations of human society.' John Adams and John Quincy Adams aren't the same person, are they?"

"No," John grinned. "John Adams was our second President, and John Quincy Adams, his son, was our sixth."

"That's right. I knew that," Thomas replied.

"All right," John said, "you've read quite a bit of information. What is the common belief and principle that the men who founded this nation had?"

Thomas sat up and thought for a minute. His answer was just forming in his head when he started his reply.

"All believed that a government could not operate effectively unless God and biblical principles were followed, that they are inseparable."

"And?"

"And that the Christian faith was instrumental in the forming of this nation."

"Very good, Tom. Simply stated, this is a Christian nation."

"But that does not make sense. If this country is supposed to be a Christian nation, why did they include the separation of church and state clause when they were giving us our rights in the Constitution?"

John had anticipated this question. He knew Thomas had been educated in a public school. John, who had been home schooled, was never impressed with his friends, who had gone through the public education system—especially when it came to the subject of history. John wasn't aware of it, but he was about to hear something that would solidify his perception. John answered Thomas's question with a question.

CHAPTER 2

· ·

DECEPTIONS
REVEALED

S o you believe that the Constitution gives us our rights? What do you know about the Declaration of Independence?" John asked.

"It was written when we were losing the war. The leaders wrote it to boost the morale of the troops. Other than that, it had no real value."

John stared at Thomas with his mouth agape in stunned disbelief. "You're joking, right?"

Thomas was baffled and a bit irritated at John's reaction.

"No, the only need for the Declaration was to boost the morale of the soldiers and keep them in the army at Valley Forge. Other than that, it serves no real purpose."

John couldn't believe his ears. He had never heard that before. "So what document made us a nation?" asked John.

"The Constitution," Thomas answered.

"Where on earth did you hear that?"

Thomas was taken aback. The overt disgust in John's tone made Thomas think about what he had just said. Why was John's reaction so strong? Thomas's irritation subsided a little.

John was Thomas's senior by about two and half years, and he stood about six foot two. But he was slender with the build of a long distance runner. Thomas was about five inches shorter than John, a little over five feet nine and a half, but had a heavier frame with hardly any fat. When he and the others worked out at the gym, Thomas easily out-lifted John. Thomas liked the weights and his body showed it. Combine that with neatly trimmed, brunette hair, deep blue eyes, and boyish looks, he was the one in the group that attracted the looks from the girls.

John, no slouch himself, had a more rugged masculine face. But more than that, he had a commanding presence about him that Thomas had rarely seen. John was not one who liked to take the lead role. For the most part, when their clique planned an activity, John was happy to go along with the consensus, letting the others decide. He seemed content participating in a variety of activities. But if arguments arose, or if a situation became difficult, then John took charge and the group listened. John had a knack for finding compromises to soothe both sides in an argument. He brought a calming effect to a time of chaos. At this time his countenance demanded attention.

Thomas responded to John's question. "Well, Phil, my senior year history teacher at Columbine…" Thomas was from Littleton, Colorado.

"Phil?"

"Well, Phil didn't want us to call him Mr. Maroon be-cause he didn't like a stuffy learning environment," Thomas answered.

"Uh-huh, and I bet Phil also taught you that there is no such thing as absolute truth and that we evolved from swamp scum, didn't he?"

Thomas reflected, "Well, yeah, he did."

"OK, Tom, I need you to have a very open mind right now. First let's look at absolute truth. Grab that dictionary from the stand over there. I'll get mine out of my pack."

Thomas walked across the room and retrieved the large *Webster's Dictionary*. The cover said, *American Dictionary of the English Language,* Noah Webster 1828. John pulled out his student dictionary, *The American Heritage Dictionary of the English Language,* and said to Thomas, "Look up *truth.*"

Thomas thumbed through the pages and found the word. John found it in his dictionary as well. "How does your dictionary define '*truth*'?" asked John.

"There are thirteen definitions. Do you want me to read them all?"

"Sure, they're short."

"Okay." Thomas read, "'One: conformity to fact or reality; exact accordance with what is, or had been, or shall be. We rely on the truth of the scriptural prophecies.' Wow! I've never seen a dictionary that talked about Scripture before!"

As he pointed to the dictionary, John said, "That's because that's a copy of the original dictionary. Remember what we just read about the other founding fathers? God was very much a part of all aspects of American life. At least for the educated portion. Go ahead and keep reading."

Thomas continued, "'Two: true state of facts or things. The duty of a court of justice is to discover the truth.'"

"Notice that truth is singular there," John cut in. He motioned for Thomas to continue.

"'Three: conformity of words to thoughts, which is called moral truth. Four: veracity; purity from falsehood.'" Thomas looked up to see if John wanted to comment.

"Go ahead to five."

"Correct opinion."

Thomas looked to John, who said, "You noticed it says 'correct opinion?' You think maybe Noah indicates that an incorrect opinion is not the truth?"

"Maybe," Thomas agreed and read on, "'Six: fidelity; constancy. Seven: honesty; virtue. Eight: exactness; conformity to rule. Nine: real fact or just principle; real state of things. Ten: sincerity.' The example they have here is interesting. I'm going to read it. 'God is a spirit, and they that worship him must worship in spirit and in truth. John 4.'"

John nodded to him.

Thomas continued, "'Eleven: the truth of God is His veracity and faithfulness. Twelve: Jesus Christ is called the truth, John 14. Thirteen: It is sometimes used by way of concession. She said, truth, Lord: yet the dogs eat of the crumbs, Matthew 15.' Wow! They used a lot of biblical references in the old days."

"Yes, they did," John replied. "Remember this, and later I'll ask you to guess when the change occurred. Now let me read what my modern dictionary has to say about truth. Not so many definitions and shorter. Let's see how well they match up. I like the first definition. 'Conformity to knowledge, fact, actuality, or logic.' I'd say that one matched up pretty well."

"Yeah," Thomas agreed.

"'Fidelity to an original or standard.' Next is 'reality; actuality.' Next 'a statement proven to be or accepted as true.' Finally 'sincerity; integrity.' I want to look up 'true.'" John quickly glanced at the other page. He read to himself then said, "I'm just going to read out loud the first and

30

third definitions. 'Consistent with fact, reality; not false or erroneous.' And 'reliable; accurate.' Okay, I'm going to make up a one-line definition to sum up all we've read, and you tell me if you think it's accurate. Truth is the accumulation of facts and evidence that provides a consistent, logical conclusion. From the definitions we've just read, would you say that is accurate?"

Thomas gave it some thought then said, "Yeah, I'd say that is a pretty accurate statement."

"Okay, now tell me what Phil, the hip teacher, told you about absolute truth."

Thomas felt compelled to get this right. He wanted his answer to be as close as possible to the way Phil had taught it to show that he knew what he was talking about. He felt his pause to organize his thoughts took minutes, but John waited patiently as he formed his answer. He finally said, "Truth is only relative to how an individual perceives his environment and events and is based on Einstein's theory of relativity."

John scrunched his face and exclaimed, "Einstein's theory of relativity is a mathematical equation that explains the relative distance between two objects in space using the speed of light as a constant! What on earth does that have to do with a personal perception?"

John's harsh tone left Thomas with a blank expression upon his face. Had he gotten it right? He was sure Phil mentioned Einstein's theory when he taught the class. Yes, he had, but for the life of him, he couldn't remember if he had ever quoted the theory or not. No, he had not.

John reiterated, "Well, how does the mathematical equation explaining the motion of objects in space coordinate with what a person thinks he sees?"

Thomas didn't have an answer.

John did not make him suffer long. Instead, in a nicer tone, he asked, "OK, how did Phil explain his statement?"

Better, Thomas thought. Phil's explanations convinced Thomas that he was right.

"All right," he looked around and spotted a picture with blue trim between the frame and picture. "See that painting on the wall over there? What color would you call the trim?"

John looked for a second, shrugged his shoulders, and said, "Some shade of blue."

"Well," Thomas asked, "what shade of blue would you call it?"

"I don't know. I'm no artist; it's just some shade of blue. That much I'm sure of."

"Well, just take a guess what color you would call it," Thomas pressed him.

"Tom, I've already answered you. It's a shade of blue. The exact shade, I don't know. But if you had a color chart with the names of the various colors on it, I could match that trim to the color chart, and then I would have enough facts to tell you what shade of blue. But, as far as the truth is concerned, I only know enough to know that it is some shade of blue."

That didn't go well. John was supposed to name the shade he thought it was, then he would tell John what shade he thought it was. He wanted to show how, although they may have named it differently, they were both right because both just perceived the colors differently because of their different experiences in life.

Figures John would mess up a simple thing like that, Thomas thought to himself. Then he remembered another example Phil had given in his class. Even John couldn't mess up this one.

"All right, let me give you another example. You'll like this one. Let's say you're a cop and you come upon the scene of an accident where a car collided with a tree. Thirty witnesses—all good, honest folks—when questioned, give you thirty different explanations of what happened, all truly believing what they say they saw happened. Are they lying to you?"

"At least twenty-nine of them are and quite possibly the thirtieth as well."

"What do you mean?" Thomas objected. "They all believed what they were saying was the truth."

"Tom, remember the definition of truth? Consistent, logical conclusions. If thirty people give thirty different stories of how an accident occurred, there is no consistency. No consistency, no truth. If they are not telling the truth, they are lying. Simple logic."

Thomas shook his head in frustration. *Why wasn't John getting this?*

"No, they believed what they were saying so in their own minds they were telling the truth. It's just how they perceived the truth."

John shook his head, "Wrong! It's how they perceived the accident. Just because a person believes a false interpretation does not make that interpretation true. Let me give you an example. Let's say I'm mad at you and I tell a lie about you to five people. Let's say I tell them that you are a pedophile and that you have had sex with five-year-old boys."

"No, we'll not go there!" interrupted Thomas.

"This is just an example, and as I said, it's a lie." John could see Thomas was uncomfortable with the subject but continued. "Now these five people have no reason *not* to believe me, and each of them tells five more people who in turn tell five more. Soon 155 people firmly believe that you are a pederast. Now, because those people firmly believe a lie started by me, does this make you a pederast?"

"No!" Thomas blurted.

"But you just said that the people at the accident scene told the truth when they gave me false information just because they believed it. So if the people who believe you're a pederast tell me as a cop that you're a pederast who has molested five-year-old boys, I should believe them too, right?"

Thomas felt trapped. What had seemed so logical now seemed preposterous. "No, as a cop you should gather all the facts to find out the truth."

"Ah, so what you're telling me now is that just because someone believes something to be true does not mean it is the truth, correct?"

"Correct!" Thomas conceded.

"Relative truth—kind of a stupid philosophy when you think about it, isn't it? Let's look up one more word." John opened his dictionary. "I'll read this to you. 'Opinion: a belief, conclusion, or judgment not substantiated by positive knowledge or proof.' It is also a 'prevailing feeling or sentiment.' You see, they are trying to sell, and have sold, the idea that an opinion is as good as the truth; that they are really the same thing. I've also seen a television commercial, one of those public service propaganda infomercials, advocating that everyone's beliefs are of equal value. So if one person believes that all persons are created equal, and another person believes the antithesis, such as that women are second-class citizens and are here strictly for the pleasure of men and to produce babies, both opinions have equal value. Obviously that's not true."

"Why would anyone want to do that?" Thomas asked. "Make people believe that an opinion and the truth are the same thing?"

"Good question. I'd like to answer it later, if you don't mind. Let me make one last statement before we move on. All truth, without exception, is absolute. It can be no other way."

Relative truth! Thomas inwardly berated himself. *How could I have been so gullible to believe such garbage? When you give it just a little thought, you can see how idiotic it is. How could I have believed it for so long?* As if John knew what he was thinking, he answered Thomas's question.

"So you trusted Phil's lie to you about the truth. Let's see if what he told you about the Declaration of Independence holds up." John picked up the history book they had read from earlier. He put that down, got up, and strode toward the history section of the library. He came back a couple of minutes later with a thin book titled, *Why America is Free.* He opened it up to chapter thirteen, "Valley Forge."

"Your Mr. Phil told you that the Declaration was written to boost the morale of the troops at Valley Forge, right?"

"Yeah, that's what he said."

"What year was the Declaration adopted?"

"July 4, 1776," Thomas answered.

"Read this and tell me when the American army was in Valley Forge."

Thomas read for a few minutes, looked up with a frown, and said, "They were there from December 1777 to March 1778. About two years after they wrote the Declaration."

John smiled and said, "Yep! Amazing, the prophetic ability of the leaders of the Revolution. But you'd think if they could have prophesied the need for a feel-good memo, they would have prophesied the need for better clothing, more food, and better shelter at Valley Forge as well. I want you to look up two more dates. One, the date when France recognized us as a nation; the other, when the Constitution was ratified."

"I just read that the French signed a treaty with us in February 1778. Is that the first date you're looking for?"

"Yes," John nodded as he opened the book to the contents. "Here, chapter seventeen. Skim through this to see if you can find when the Constitution was ratified."

Thomas read silently for several minutes.

"This was interesting. I learned some things I didn't know before."

"Did you find the date?" John asked.

"I think so. It kind of gives two dates. New Hampshire voted on it on June 21, 1788, and New York voted on it on July 26 of that same year."

"My text says it was ratified on July 2, 1788, so New Hampshire must have been the state to give it the three-fourths majority it needed. So if the Constitution made us a nation, what were we between the time we started and finished the Revolutionary War and the time the Constitution was enacted? We're talking close to ten years."

Thomas just shook his head.

"Have you ever been to a federal office building?" John asked.

"No."

"I have an aunt who works in the one in Billings. In the lobby is a display with copies of the Declaration, the Constitution, and the Bill of Rights. The Declaration is positioned in the center and above, with the Constitution at the lower right and the Bill of Rights at the lower left. Why do you think the Declaration is in the position of honor?"

Thomas was not slow. When facts were clearly given, he was quick to grasp the obvious.

"Because it is the most important document of the three."

"Very good! So do you think Phil was teaching the straight scoop when he told you the Declaration of Independence was just a feel-good memo for the troops?"

"No, but why would he lie about a thing like that?"

"If you stay with me until the end, I'm sure you'll have your answer. Although," John smiled, "I'll bet you're not going to like the answer. Now let's get back to your question that got us on this tangent. You asked, 'Why would the founders, who were obviously Christians, add a separation of church and state clause in the Constitution?' You also indicated that you believed that the Constitution gave us our rights. First I want to address where our rights originate. That's why I asked you about the Declaration of Independence." John picked up the original history book from which they had read and opened to a copy of the Declaration of Independence. "Here it is," John said. "Read the second paragraph out loud please."

While Thomas took the book, John reached for another. Thomas read, "'We hold these truths to be self-evident, that all men are created equal, that they are endowed by their Creator with certain unalienable rights.'"

"That's good," John interrupted. "Where do our rights come from?"

"God."

"That's right." John handed Thomas the other book, one they had already used that morning, and said, "Now read this quote by John F. Kennedy."

"'The rights of man come not from the generosity of the state, but from the Hand of God.'"

"Have you ever read the Constitution?" John asked.

Thomas raised an eyebrow and said, "No! Are we about to go off on another tangent?"

"Maybe, maybe not," John smiled. "We'll be looking at the Constitution a lot today. I just want you to read the preamble to the Bill of Rights for now."

Thomas wore a puzzled look on his face. "I didn't know the Bill of Rights had a preamble."

"Most people don't. You won't find it in most history books. I printed this copy from a government website. Just read the second paragraph."

"'The convention of number of the states, having at the time of their adopting the Constitution, expressed a desire, in order to prevent misconstruction or abuse of its powers, that further declaratory and restrictive clauses should be added.'"

"That's good right there," John cut in. "You see, the Constitution was never designed to give people their rights. It never did and it never will. The Constitution doesn't even govern the people. It has no sway over you and me as private citizens. It's a document that governs the government, and the Bill of Rights is designed to protect us *from* the government."

"I read something to that effect in the *Why America is Free* book while I was looking up the date of the Constitution. A guy from Virginia—George Mason, I think—wanted a Bill of Rights to protect the people from tyranny."

"Good, very good!" John nodded. "Let's go to the church and state issue. Nowhere in the Constitution is there a separation of church and state. It's a lie by the courts."

That was an eye-opener for Thomas—literally. His eyes opened wide and his head jerked back. At this time a young man entered the library and made eye contact with John. He nodded a greeting and watched as the student, whom John had seen on campus before, went between the bookshelves in search of the desired material. John glanced at his watch, which read 8:10.

"Let's take a potty break and stretch our legs."

"Sounds like a good idea to me," Thomas agreed. Both got up and headed to the hallway, making their way to the restroom. Thomas seemed a little downcast. After relieving themselves, they started to walk the hallways.

"You must think I'm pretty stupid," Thomas finally said.

"Stupid? Why?"

Thomas's eyes showed his dejection. "Because I believed in relative truth and didn't even know what the Declaration was about."

"No, Tom. I don't think you're stupid. Quite the contrary. What we're talking about and the things that I'm about to tell you are not for the weak-minded. A simpleton couldn't understand the things we're going to discuss much less figure out 'who done it'. No! If I thought you didn't have the intellect for complex thought, I wouldn't have even invited you here today. Do I think you're stupid? Deceived? Definitely. But don't feel bad about letting yourself be deceived. Those who did it are masters of deception and manipulation. They've had years of practice and know every nuance of the art."

"Who are they?"

John just smiled at Thomas and said, "That is a question to be answered later in the day. Also, I don't want you to think that my having you read material is to belittle you. I just want you to see firsthand that all I'm telling you is historically true. I'm not giving you my opinion without having the evidence to back it up."

"Okay," answered Thomas. He thought about what John had just said about his being deceived. That was exactly how he felt, deceived and betrayed. He wondered, *If this much of my education has been lies, how much of my education can I trust? Was any of it true? Exactly how educated am I?*

He always considered himself a good student with a high B average. He didn't question his ability to learn as much as he questioned the legitimacy of the subject matter he had been taught. His mind drifted to *The Tonight Show* with Jay Leno and his "Jay Walking" segment. Leno visits different college campuses and asks students some of the easiest questions from American history to current events. These knuckleheads, as he used to think of them, came up with the stupidest answers. Now Thomas wondered if he would be one of those knuckleheads.

"Are you ready to get started again?" John asked.

"Huh?" The question dragged Thomas from his thoughts.

"Are you ready to get started again? Do you even want to continue?"

"Yes, I'm ready and yes, I want to see this through to the end," Thomas replied in a determined tone. "You've definitely sparked my interest."

John had said that the weak-minded would not be able to comprehend what he was talking about. Thomas felt the need to prove to himself, and to John, that he was anything but weak-minded. Thomas wasn't sure where the trail led, but he would stay with it. John had said this was developing motive. But the fact that America had its roots founded in Christianity seemed the most unlikely motive he could think of. It was still early, and John said they would be done around three o'clock, so more information would surely follow. He wondered how much more he would have to read. He would rather have had the material made into a movie.

CHAPTER 3

ASSASSINATION

They settled back down in their chairs. John began, "So far this probably feels more like schoolwork than a game."

"Yeah, kind of," Thomas answered.

"Yeah, and it's horrible to do schoolwork on a Saturday, but detective work is a lot like schoolwork. You just have to think a little harder. Or so my father used to tell me. So far, we've looked at background information that will help establish motive—more for the genocide that I believe is about to occur rather than the old genocide that we will concentrate on now. We still need to look up some history."

"More reading?"

"Yes, a lot more reading."

"Oh!" Thomas faked a moan.

John playfully slapped his head. "I told you I want you to see the evidence for yourself and not just take my word for it. I would be a secondhand witness, and secondhand testimonial is not permissible in a court of law. So you see,

41

detective, you have to read. Where was I? Ah, yeah, now we have to look at the beginnings of the Democratic party."

"The Democratic party! This must be a clue. So was the victim a Democrat, or was the killer?"

"The victim most definitely; the killer claimed to be. May I go on?"

"Sure." Thomas raised his head and waved his hand as if giving John permission.

"Thank you! Tell me, who founded the Democratic party?"

Uh-oh, Thomas thought. *Thanks, Phil.*

"I have no idea," he responded.

"Andrew Jackson," John answered.

"I would have guessed Jefferson." Thomas felt the need to show John he knew some history.

"That would have been a good guess," John replied. "Thomas Jefferson was the first President from the Democratic-Republican party. At one time they were one and the same. But the issue of slavery divided the party into two groups, the Whigs and the Democrats. Just before the Civil War the issue of slavery came up again, and the Whig party split into Whigs and Republicans. The Republicans wanted to free the slaves. It's probably best to start off with Jefferson because it was his principles by which Jackson formed and groomed the Democratic party. Jefferson believed in democracy, the Greek version of democracy, meaning the will of the people or people's rule. He once said, 'Give the people light and they will find their own way.' He developed the theory of states' rights, which was against giving the federal government much authority. He also believed that laws were to be made by those who are to obey them."

"I thought Congress made them," Thomas replied.

"Yeah, I guess that they never heard of Jefferson's theory," John laughed. "Anyway, Jefferson believed in individual rights, religious freedom, freedom of speech, intellectual inquiry, and the freedom of the press. He didn't even relent in his belief in the freedom of the press when they wrote a bunch of slanderous stories about him. Jackson ardently believed in these principles when he molded the Democratic party. They believed in the will, and I emphasize *will*, of the people. I want you to read an insert I found about Jackson and Truman. Read this from here to the end of the paragraph."

John handed Thomas the book. Before reading he looked at the top left page, *Persecution*. Thomas thought that this might be something of a clue. He read, "'Columnist Dave Kopel, in National Review Online, wrote of two of America's greatest Democratic Presidents doing just that.'" Thomas paused, saying, "That does not make sense. Doing just what?"

"I'm sorry, Tom," John grimaced. "I should have had you start with the line before that."

Thomas read, "'Also heavily relied on God for strength in times of crisis and difficulty.' Okay, that's better." He continued, "'The founder of the Democratic party, Andrew Jackson, explained Kopel, was a Presbyterian who read his Bible daily and "applied its principles directly" in handling his most difficult struggle as President, involving the Second Bank of the United States. In announcing his decision to veto a bill to recharter the bank in 1832, Jackson used biblical imagery as he did later on in the crisis when he said, "I will not bow down to the golden calf." And just when he was about to cave in to pressure from opponents, he heard church bells ringing, went to church, and recovered his determination to fight. Similarly, Kopel detailed the role President Harry Truman's Southern Baptist faith played in his Israel policy. Kopel concluded, "While the Jackson and Truman presidencies were not perfect, they were at their best when Jackson and Truman were inspired to follow eternal standards of morality rather than political expediency.""

Thomas thought to himself, *This doesn't sound like the Democratic party I know.* John watched Thomas as if he could see his mind working.

"Are you following along okay?"

Thomas just nodded his head.

"Good, because we're about to come to the first death, and I want you to be concentrating closely enough to catch it as well as the assassin."

Thomas racked his brain, trying to remember which presidents had been assassinated. He could remember only two, Abraham Lincoln and John F. Kennedy. But only Kennedy was a Democrat. He was sure he knew what was going to happen next. Kennedy was president in the fifties or sixties, sometime around then. Yeah, he was ready for John. *Come on! Bring it on,* he thought.

John grabbed still another very thick book and continued, "Let me set the scene for you. About three years before the death in question, on October 24, a day known as Black Tuesday, the stock market took a dive. It crashed. Naturally this was very upsetting for most people. There were a lot of knee-jerk reactions, such as runs on the banks, and in the subsequent chaos our nation was plunged into what was known as the Great Depression."

"Sounds depressing," Thomas interjected.

"You'd think so, but the depression pulled people together. During the early twenties America's prosperity was at its greatest since its birth. With modern conveniences, such as quick communication with the telephone and greater mobility with the automobile, life was easy. People started to indulge in the pleasures of life. That's why it was called the 'Roaring Twenties.' This is when the 'me' generation got its birth. People developed the philosophy of 'I'll do what's pleasing for me and forget about anyone else.' But when the depression came, that self-assurance and arrogance yielded to uncertainty and humility. People realized that we need to be able to depend on each other and work together.

"My grandmother told me that while she was a kid, she never knew there was a depression. One family grew one kind of crop, another family grew a different type of crop, and they would trade. If a man was sick and couldn't work his field, the men of the community came together after they were done in their fields and worked the sick man's field. If a man was good at plumbing and a family needed help with their plumbing, he'd go help them. Not only did people learn to depend on each other, but more people started to go to church. The needy found relief at their religious institutions."

"It sounds like Bush's faith-based initiative," said Thomas.

"Yeah, maybe we should have another depression to kick that off."

"Not!" Both said at the same time.

"Anyway," John continued, "let's get back to the first death. With the depression, one out of every four persons was without a job, the banks were in shambles, and everyone looked to the president to save the day."

John had ended that last sentence with enough sarcasm to make Thomas question him. "The way you said that makes it sound like you don't think it's his job. Isn't it?"

John shook his head and said, "Nope, not at all." John dug through his pile of books and pulled out a stapled stack of papers. Thomas could tell that he had used these worn pages before. "I got this off the web, from a government website. It's the Constitution in its entirety. Article Two covers the executive branch. Section One talks about how a president is elected, eligibility requirements, and terms. The second and third sections tell what his duties are and the extent of his authority. Read these two sections to yourself, then show me where it's the responsibility of the president to take charge of the economic well-being of this nation."

Thomas took the pages. "So you don't want me to read this out loud? There isn't much here."

"No. Just when you're done, show me where he's responsible for the economy."

John sat back and relaxed while Thomas read the three short paragraphs.

"That's it? That's all the authority the president has?" Thomas asked.

"Yep, that's it. So can you point out where it says the president is responsible for the economic welfare of this nation?"

"There has to be more somewhere in the Constitution about other duties, isn't there?"

"Well, yes," John conceded. "Article One gives him the authority to sign a bill into law and the power of the veto. But other than that, he's allowed to do only what these two sections say he can do."

Thomas looked perplexed. "Well, then, why do we expect the president to solve all the world's problems?"

"Ignorance!" John said. "The founders of this nation were political geniuses, the likes of which haven't been seen in decades. Even though it's plainly written for people, they still don't understand the governmental hierarchy set out in the Constitution. People basically want a king, one person to whom they can turn in times of trouble. Actually a monarchy is the most efficient form of government with only one problem."

"What's that?"

"Monarchs! In all the history of mankind you could probably count the really great kings on one hand. Many have had their shining moments but still have fallen short of the mark. So when America has a problem, whatever the problem, they turn to the president. I admit that the treaties the president makes have an effect on our economy, and a good president will draft treaties to our economic benefit. Setting up trade agreements and proper tariffs is good, but for the day to day economic affairs of the nation, the president should have no involvement."

"Then who should?"

"The people or the state governments," John responded.

"Is that anywhere in the Constitution?"

"Yep." John took the Constitution from Thomas, turned the pages, then handed it back to him. "Read the Tenth Amendment out loud."

"'The powers not delegated to the United States by the Constitution, nor prohibited by it to the States, are reserved to the States respectively or to the people.' Well, I'll be."

"You see, the President, Congress, and the Supreme Court can act only on things that fall within the confines of the Constitution. All other matters are the responsibility of the states and/or the people. The people have a lot more power than just voting, but you won't ever get the federal government to admit that. Shall we get off this tangent and get back to the subject at hand?"

"No," Thomas said. "I have one other question I'd like to ask you." John nodded and listened. "When I read about the president's duties, I noticed Section Four where it talks about impeachment. It said a president could be impeached for a misdemeanor." Thomas paused to look for confirmation that John knew what he was talking about.

"Yeah," John said patiently, waiting for him to form his question.

"Well, I remember when Clinton was impeached. Some senators said that the only reason a president could be impeached was for treason."

"Were they Republicans or Democrats?"

"Democrats, I think," said Thomas.

"They lied, go figure," John chided. Thomas waited. He obviously wanted more of an answer. "The Constitution states that the president, vice president, and *all* civil officers of the United States, shall be removed from office on impeachment for conviction of treason, bribery, or other high crimes and misdemeanors. High crimes are felonies. You should note the word *shall*, meaning this is not supposed to be optional. Our federal leaders are supposed to be held to the highest standard of conduct. Anytime a congressman, judge, or the president or vice president commits a crime, he is supposed to be impeached."

"But they aren't," Thomas said.

"No, they work on the good ol' boy system. You've heard of the code of silence with cops, right?"

"Yeah."

"It's the same thing. You look the other way when I do something wrong, and I'll look the other way when you do something wrong. We call it politics."

"But that ain't right!"

"No," John agreed.

"Isn't there something in the Constitution that permits congressmen to break the law?" Thomas asked.

"Article One, Section Six."

"How do you know these things off the top of your head like that?"

"I started studying the Constitution in high school for a paper," John smiled. "I liked it so much that I kept with it. Guess it comes from being a cop's son. Anyway I know Articles One, Two, and Three and the Bill of Rights pretty well and the rest of the Constitution fairly well. Let me show you that section."

John took the papers, turned to the appropriate page, and pointed to a section. Sure enough, it was six. He pointed to a part and showed Thomas where to read.

"'They shall in all cases, except treason, felony, and breach of the peace, be privileged from arrest during their attendance at the session of their respective Houses, and in going to and returning from the same.' A breach of the peace is a misdemeanor, isn't it?"

"Yep."

"Well, what else is there?"

"Petty offenses, torts punishable under thirty days. Remember when the Constitution was first written? They had to go from town to town on horseback. Well, you couldn't expect a representative to know all the ordinances in every town he passed. This clause was put in so he wouldn't spend time in jail because his horse relieved itself on Main Street contrary to a city ordinance. Still, it does not excuse elected officials from maintaining that high standard of conduct."

Thomas nodded his understanding.

"Back to the murder?" John asked.

"Oh, yeah. That thing. Sure, let's go."

"Okay, we were talking about the depression. About one out of every four persons was out of a job, and people were getting pretty tired of it. Hoover didn't seem to be coming up with the right answers. When it came time for the next election, people were ready for some kind of change. And that is when it happened, the assassination!"

John took the heavy history book and handed it to Thomas. He opened to a pre-marked page and pointed to a story entitled, "Roosevelt Elected, Pledging New Deal."

"Here, read just the first paragraph. Let's see if you catch the assassination."

Before reading, Thomas examined the book. It looked like a collection of news articles. He read from the one John had indicated. "'Washington, D.C., Nov. 8. When Franklin D. Roosevelt exclaimed at the democratic convention that he "pledged a new deal for the American people," they believed him and took their beliefs to the polls. In an election that many experts consider the most crucial since Lincoln's victory more than seventy years ago, Roosevelt has been swept into the White House with an overwhelming plurality. The latest vote tally gives him almost 23 million to President Hoover's 15 million. Norman Thomas, the socialist candidate, collected about 885,000 votes while the communist party choice, William Foster, polled over 100,000 votes.'"

Thomas glanced at John. John just tilted his head and raised an eyebrow as if waiting for Thomas's revelation. Thomas was confused. He thought he was looking for an assassination, not an election.

"Is this all you wanted me to read?"

"Uh-huh," John replied.

Thomas turned back to the book and read silently to himself. He read the paragraph again, then the rest of the news article. It talked a bit about Roosevelt's background and some of his campaign promises. The one part that caught his attention was that in his campaign he first proposed a 25 percent cut in government spending, then turned around and said he would consider deficit spending. *Typical politician,* Thomas thought. Still, there was nothing about a murder, let alone a group of them.

Thomas turned the page and found three more news articles about Roosevelt. The third was titled, "Roosevelt Escapes Assassin's Bullet." He read that article. The mayor of Chicago, Anton Cermak, was killed, but Roosevelt escaped.

"John, is this the article you meant for me to read?" Thomas pointed it out, and John glanced over.

"No, the one I gave you to read is here on this page." John turned the page back to where he had it.

"But there is no murder on this page!"

"Yes," John replied, "in sorts there was."

"In sorts?"

"When Roosevelt was inaugurated and implemented the New Deal, he killed the Democratic party—what it represented, its principles—and he established socialism. The philosophy went from the will of the people to the well-being of the people as we see fit."

"Hold on, John. That is not murder. I know what a murder is. It's the unlawful act of taking a human life with malice aforethought." John was impressed. That was the legal definition of murder. Thomas continued, "You can't kill a political idea!"

"We've called this a genocide."

"Yes, but genocide is the killing off a race of people, right?" Thomas corrected him.

John took his dictionary and skimmed through the pages, then read to Thomas, "Genocide—the systematic annihilation of a racial, political, or cultural group." John emphasized both political and cultural. "Technically you're probably right. The definition is probably referring to the actual killing of the people in those groups, but Sam and I couldn't find a word that meant killing off one political party's philosophy for another surreptitiously. Genocide is as close as we can get. In reality that is what Roosevelt did. He assassinated the ideas and policies of Jefferson and Jackson and deceitfully established socialism. He went from the will of the people to the well-being of the people as we see it."

Thomas nodded. He was willing to relent on the technical definition of the word since he did not know of any other word that defined that situation, and the fact that John had admitted that he was right.

"Roosevelt's New Deal was nothing more than social-ism," John continued. "He knew it and so did most of the Republican party. Hoover even criticized him for it. Person-ally what I don't like about it was that he should have run under the socialist ballot instead of Norman Thomas, but he was too brilliant for that."

"Brilliant? Why call him brilliant for a deception?" Thomas was appalled.

"It is obvious that Roosevelt understood human nature. Americans back then, as they do fairly much today, con-sidered themselves independent. The democratic process appeals to that spirit of free will. So by calling himself a Democrat and keeping the title Democrat for his new party, he started off with a large following and a firm foundation. His timing was perfect. He couldn't have asked for a better social climate than the one he had. If there wasn't a depres-sion going on, he couldn't have been elected with that cam-paign. But there was, and the people were receptive to just about any policy that would help them out of it. A new deal sounded good. The people were not interested in a political technicality. He becomes president and this nation becomes socialist. I want to show you a list of government agencies. Hand me that *Compton's Encyclopedia* by you."

Thomas handed it to him. The page was marked with a piece of paper.

"Here, count the number of agencies Roosevelt established while he was president."

Thomas looked at the list, which took up the whole page. It was covered with acronyms. He counted them, then said, "Wow—thirty-five."

"Yeah," John said, "that's what you call government domination. Roosevelt asked for broad powers, and

Congress gave it to him. I want you to read some of these agencies in this list and see what they did."

He pointed to one and Thomas read, "'CCC—Civilian Conservation Corps, created in 1933 to succeed the agency known as Emergency Conservation Work; to provide employment and vocational training for needy young men through work in the conservation and development of natural resources. In Federal Security Agency until abolished in 1942.'"

John pointed to another.

Thomas continued to read, "'FCC (Federal Communications Commission) created in 1934 to regulate interstate and foreign communications by telegraph, telephone, cable, and radio. FERA (Federal Emergency Relief Administration) created in 1933 to relieve the hardships caused by unemployment and drought. Abolished in 1938 and its work carried on by WPA until 1942. FWA (Federal Works Agency) created in 1939 to coordinate all public construction. NHA (National Housing Agency) created in 1942 to consolidate all housing activities. FSA (Farm Security Administration) created in 1937 to aid tenant farmers and to carry on rehabilitation work of Resettlement Administration. SEC (Securities and Exchange Commission) created in 1934 to license and regulate stock exchange and to control public utility holding companies. SSB (Social Security Board) created in 1935 to administer the federal old-age retirement funds.'"

John interrupted and said, "Finally I want you to read this one. I like the way it ends." John pointed to the last agency he wanted Thomas to read about.

Thomas read, "'TVA (Tennessee Valley Authority) created in 1933 to operate government-owned properties at Muscle Shoals, Alabama; to develop water and power resources of the Tennessee River watershed; to plan for the social and economic well-being of the valley.'"

"Do you know what the definition of socialism is?" John asked.

"Yes, it's an organized group that holds both political power and production and distribution means."

John was impressed. "Very good. Can that definition be applied to what we just read?"

Thomas nodded his head and said, "Yeah, it most certainly can."

"It's a long ways from what Jefferson said about government. 'That government is best which governs least,'" quoted John.

"Uh-huh. Are any of those agencies still active?" Thomas asked.

"The Social Security Board is part of the Social Security Administration. You've heard of the FCC; they're still around and called by that same name.

Thomas replied, "Yeah, I have heard of them."

John continued, "Most were absorbed by newer agencies. A few were abandoned because the Supreme Court declared two of Roosevelt's laws unconstitutional. They were the Agriculture Adjustment Act, where the government paid farmers and ranchers not to produce anything, and National Recovery Acts, which controlled wages and prices and limited competition among businesses while encouraging labor organizations, better known as unions."

"So how were these laws unconstitutional?"

"Practically everything Roosevelt did was unconstitutional. I don't know the actual argument the Supreme Court used, but I can show you in the Constitution why I can say that."

"Okay, I'm game," Thomas said.

"Where did we put that copy of the Constitution?"

Thomas and John dug under the pile of books at their table. John quickly came up with the document and found the part of the Constitution he was looking for.

"This is Article Four," John continued. "It recognizes the power and authority given to the state. I want you to read Section One and the first sentence in Section Two."

"'Section One. Full faith and credit shall be given in each State to the public Acts,...'"

John interrupted, "I want you to see how that is written. Notice that Acts is capitalized and followed by a comma. This is a list of the state's authority. All three are separate functions. Go ahead."

"'The public Acts, Records, and judicial Proceedings of every other State. And the Congress may by general Laws prescribe the Manner in which such Acts, Records, and Proceeding shall be proved, and the effect thereof. Section Two. The citizens of each State shall be entitled to all Privileges and Immunities of Citizens in the several States.'" Thomas finished.

"Okay, Tom, what does the term 'full faith and credit' mean to you?"

"That they are given all the responsibility to provide for the things listed below."

"Good. Is the federal government reserving any power to do the same things?"

"No! The responsibilities are fully on the states. But the federal government does reserve the right to make the states prove they are making the appropriate laws and the effectiveness of those laws," Thomas answered.

"Very astute," John said. "Okay, what then are public acts?"

"Any dealings that affect the people."

"Such as?"

Thomas thought for a couple of minutes then said, "Education, health, employment, welfare, housing ordinances—anything that might affect people."

"Very good," John nodded. "How about Records?"

Thomas had to rack his brain a little harder on this one. He looked the section over again. He knew that John was going to ask him about judicial proceedings next, and he wasn't sure at all what that meant. After a little longer pause than his first one, he answered, "Records would be public records, such as birth certificates, drivers' licenses, taxes, and I believe, records of the state's dealings and their legislations."

"Excellent!" John exclaimed.

Before he had a chance to continue, Thomas said, "And before you ask me about judicial proceedings, let me tell you, I don't have a clue what they're talking about."

"It has two meanings," John said. "First that the states are responsible for their own judicial proceedings, court cases, and second…"John stopped for a second to form his explanation in the easiest way he could think of, then continued, "If a judge in one state handed down a certain ruling, an attorney in a different state defending a client on similar charges may present that ruling to the presiding judge as a precedent for his client. So states can use other states' rulings to help them with difficult decisions or to help expedite hearings."

"Do they have to go with that other judge's rulings?"

"No," John answered. "Each case is different with different circumstances. One state's laws may be more explicit than another, which may make the court ruling non-applicable. It's more for guidance than anything else. But in all three of these responsibilities the federal government is not supposed to interfere with the state's rights. Take a look at all of those agencies Roosevelt started. What do each of them do in respect to the state's rights?"

Thomas looked at the list again and it became apparent. "They all violate the public acts portion of the Constitution!" Thomas exclaimed.

John just smiled. He knew Thomas was bright. Then he asked, "Do you want to hear the ruling by the Supreme Court that gave them the authority to declare a law unconstitutional? It's significant."

Thomas did not hesitate. "Sure," he said.

John took the document containing the Constitution and turned to the last page. There he had typed additional footnotes containing court cases, one of which was the case that he wanted Thomas to hear now.

"I'll read this to you," John said. "'In 1803, the Supreme Court established its power to declare an act of Congress unconstitutional. The case, *Marbury v. Madison,* involved an act of Congress which enlarged the original jurisdiction of the Supreme Court. The Court said that a law which is repugnant to the Constitution is void, and the Congress lacked the power to enlarge or decrease the Supreme Court's original jurisdiction.'" After John finished he said, "You see, any law or act that violates the Constitution is to be voided. It also confirms that Congress does not have unlimited authority and must comply with the Constitution as well. The next question should be: What does Congress have the authority to pass laws on?"

"Okay," Thomas humored him, "what does Congress have the authority to pass laws on?"

"Great question! Let me answer that for you. Better yet, I'll give you the Constitution and it can answer you." Without hesitation John turned to the page he was looking for and pointed it out.

"You know, John, if I didn't know how much you liked to have a good time, I'd think you had no life at all."

"I told you I knew the first three Articles pretty well," John laughed. "Our answer is in Article One, Section Eight. Eight, by the way, is the section that outlines the vast majority of the federal government's authority. Read paragraph eighteen."

"'To make all Laws which shall be necessary and proper for carrying into Execution the foregoing Powers, and all other Powers vested by this Constitution in the Government of the United States, or in any Department or Officer thereof.' So," Thomas said after reading the paragraph, "Congress is restricted to making laws with regard to what is granted in the Constitution."

John nodded, "That's correct. Any laws made outside the confines of the Constitution are unlawful, illegal, and unconstitutional!"

"Okay," Thomas said, "if all those agencies and laws Roosevelt established were unconstitutional, why didn't the Supreme Court rule them all that way?"

"Good question. Remember the depression?" Thomas nodded, so John continued, "The economy was building, and it looked to the people like Roosevelt's incentives were working. Although judges are not supposed to play politics, they do. So they were willing to let these laws stand while the nation appeared to be recovering."

"So Roosevelt's laws worked," Thomas concluded.

"No."

"You just said they did," Thomas argued.

"No, I said the economy was building, and the people attributed it to his programs. His New Deal programs weren't making the economy work, but Roosevelt did directly help its recovery."

Thomas looked confused, so John expounded on his explanation.

"The first thing Roosevelt did when he took office was to declare a national bank holiday. This means he closed all the banks until they could get their feet back underneath them. He also had fireside chats, or radio broadcasts addressed to the public. In them, he reassured the people that their money was secure in banks and a better investment than keeping it under their mattress. Just these two things did wonders. People started to put their money in the bank. Banks were able to invest. Invested companies were able to grow. This provided jobs, and, as the economy was at rock bottom, it had no way to go but up. A lot of his initiatives did help the process, especially those that supplied jobs, but I couldn't tell you how much they offset the negative effects of socialism."

"What would some of those be?" asked Thomas.

"Well, other than a smothering amount of laws," John said, "it also required exorbitant amounts of taxes. You have to get the money somewhere to pay for all those jobs, and, with the exception of power plants the government built, the government does not provide commerce. The problem Roosevelt had was the economy was coming back too quickly for him and his party."

"Too quickly?" Thomas interjected.

"Yes, too quickly. That's why he implemented the Agriculture Adjustment Act and the National Recovery Act. One drove up food prices, making it hard for people to buy food. The other crippled industry by making it hard to turn a profit and developing strong unions. That's why the Supreme Court declared them unconstitutional."

"That makes absolutely no sense at all. Why would Roosevelt want to slow economic recovery? It just doesn't make sense," Thomas said flatly.

"Actually, it makes perfect sense and it was a great strategy. I've already told you that he and his group had an understanding of human nature. History shows that it takes about seven years to change a mind-set of a people. Roosevelt was trying to do just that. He needed at least seven years to have the American people accept his philosophy of democracy instead of the one they knew by Jefferson and Jackson. He got a little over twelve years. By then it was pretty firmly set. Had the economy sprung back too soon, the people may have revolted at all of the government control."

John stopped and watched Thomas. He could see he was deep in thought. John thought he would give him a minute before he continued with the game, but Thomas asked, "Are any of the laws and government agencies we have today unconstitutional?"

"Oh, I'd say about two-thirds of them are. Can I give you an example and show you why they're unconstitutional?"

"Yeah, I think I'd like to see that," Thomas replied.

His avid interest in their discussion encouraged John. He said, "There is a lot to choose from, but I think I will focus on national parks and national forests. Section Eight is not long. Go ahead and read it to yourself. Let me know when you get to paragraph seventeen." John pointed out the beginning of the section and Thomas began to read.

Within seconds he asked, "Here in the first paragraph, what exactly is meant by common defense and general welfare? That seems kind of vague."

"It is vague. The first paragraph is just an overview of the section. The following paragraphs explain what they mean by common defense and general welfare. Just read, you'll see."

Thomas continued and in less than a minute he said, "I'm at seventeen. Do you want me to read it out loud?" John nodded. "'To exercise exclusive Legislation in all cases whatsoever, over such District (not exceeding ten miles square) as may, by Cession of particular States, and the acceptance of Congress, become the Seat of the Government of the United States, and to exercise like Authority over all Places purchased by the Consent of the Legislature of the State in which the same shall be, for the Erection of Forts, Magazines, Arsenals, dock-yards, and other needful Buildings;' and we go into paragraph eighteen here, which I've already read."

"So can you tell me why the Park Service and Forest Service are unconstitutional?"

"To tell you the truth, John, I had some problem understanding the last paragraph. I know it's important or you wouldn't have had me read it aloud. What is meant *by cession?*"

That was a fair question. It showed that Thomas was not just blindly accepting what he heard. John explained, "By *cession* means to receive land by a treaty. The federal government can acquire land or a building from a state via a treaty or by purchasing it, and the feds would have exclusive jurisdiction over it. The key things you need to look at are the land limitations and what the land can be used for. Tell me, have you ever seen a national park or forest less than ten miles square?"

"No," Thomas said, "and it doesn't mention either of them in the list of uses either."

"That's right. Did you read anywhere else in section eight where it mentioned parks or national forests?"

"No. Is it in any other place that I haven't read?"

"No! Now apply what you've learned and tell me why they are unconstitutional."

Thomas already had an answer, but he gave it a little more thought to make sure it was as complete as he could get it. Finally, he said, "First they exceed the ten square mile limit. Then they are not listed as part of their authority; therefore, they violate the eighteenth paragraph of this section and the Tenth Amendment that says, what authority isn't given to the U.S. is reserved for the states."

"By Jove, I think he's got it!" exclaimed John, "That was excellent. Now tell me, Social Security, is it constitutional or unconstitutional, and why either way?"

Thomas immediately responded, "Unconstitutional, because it violates the public acts portion and the Tenth Amendment because it's not a responsibility designated to them by the Constitution."

"Excellent! How about the Civil Rights Act?"

"Unconstitutional for the same reasons."

"Gotcha!" John said. "Actually that is kind of a trick question. There were a couple of Civil Right Acts, one in 1960, and one in 1964 that I know of. The first one was directed at the states to ensure everyone, regardless of their race, could vote. Remember when you read Article Four and the second section?"

"Oh, yeah!" Thomas interrupted, "Citizens entitled to all privileges of the states."

"Yeah, that. It was general in nature in accordance with section one of that article. So with regard to that, it was OK. The one in 1964 went too far. Not only did it prohibit states from discriminating against voter registration, but it subjugated private industry. So it violated the Tenth Amendment, not only by overrunning the state's authority but the people's as well. So you are right about the second one."

Thomas seemed to have some mixed emotions. Thomas liked having national forests for camping and hiking, and the public lands for hunting and fishing. He hated the thought of their being private property; no trespassing signs everywhere without a chance of doing the things he loved to do. He always figured the Civil Rights Act, or what he

knew of it, was a good thing. So he asked, "John, technically, these things may be unconstitutional, but if they are
a benefit to the people, shouldn't we allow them?"

"Never," answered John. "If the Constitution is ignored
for 'the good of the people,' then our nation truly has no
foundation on which to base our laws. One abuse leads to
more, until all our rights are stripped away. Besides, the
Constitution has a way to ensure the needs of the people are
met. If the Congress or the president feels there is a need,
Article Four gives them the authority to make a general law
directing the states to develop, pass, and implement laws
that meet that need. The states are free to devise whatever
solution they deem proper for their people. The Fourth
Article also gives the federal government the authority to
pass laws requiring the states to provide proof that their
laws are effective. Should the laws prove ineffective, then
the federal government can require the states to amend
their laws so they comply with the original act. It does not
mean the federal government can usurp the state's authority and implement laws that govern the people. Remember
when I told you that the founders of this nation and the
Constitution were political geniuses?"

"Yeah," Thomas replied.

"They understood," John continued, "that when a government governs a large number of people and territory,
and it is given unlimited power, the government becomes
dictatorial and the people merely become slaves of the
state. This is the very reason why the Constitution limits
the authority it gives to the government. It is also the reason why the founders demanded a Bill of Rights—a list of
rights upon which the government could never infringe.
That's what the preamble of the Bill of Rights specifically
said. Tell me this, Tom. Is it easier for people to follow the

political happenings and therefore have a greater say in those happenings at the city or county level of government?"

"The city," Thomas answered.

"Okay, at which level is it easier for the people to stay involved in the political process, at the county or the state?"

"The county."

"And at which level is it easier for the people to stay involved in the political process, at the state or the federal?"

"At the state."

"You're correct all three times. It's simple logic. It's easier for the people to stay involved in the local communities and hardest at the federal level. Our founders clearly understood this. Did you ever hear the old adage, 'Power corrupts, absolute power corrupts absolutely'? Our founders had and they understood it. They also knew that the most effective means for the people to control the larger government was to limit its authority. That is why the Constitution is designed the way it is, so that we the people of the United States stay the true authority and remain free. Socialism and communism do just the opposite. With them the federal government is all-powerful, and local government is subject to their whims. The people are enslaved by edicts, laws, and statutes. Law: the strong-arm tactics of an abusive government. Tell me, does any of this sound familiar in regard to our present-day government?"

Thomas sat back and thought about what John had just said. This was definitely radical thinking, or was it? John always had the evidence of what he said right there before him. Maybe John was thinking conventionally, and he himself had been taught to think radically. *What a concept. This is hard enough to comprehend without muddling my own mind.*

He was deep in thought when John said, "Let me give you a little more food for thought. You've heard of TSA, haven't you?"

"Isn't that the Transportation Security Administration

"Right! They're a federal agency that searches you and your luggage as you enter the airport terminal. I want you to read the Fourth Amendment." John grabbed the Constitution.

As he searched for the right page, Thomas asked, "Didn't we already read that?"

"No," John said. "We read Article Four of the original Constitution. The Fourth Amendment is part of the Bill of Rights. Here it is. Now read this."

John handed him the papers. Thomas read, "'The right of the people to be secure in their persons, houses, papers, and effects against unreasonable searches and seizures, shall not be violated, and no warrants shall issue, but upon probable cause, supported by Oath or affirmation, and particularly describing the place to be searched, and the persons or things to be seized.'"

"Do you understand it?" John asked.

"Yes, it means that the government can't search you or your things unless they have a warrant."

"Right! No government agency, whether it's state, local, or federal, can search you or your things unless they suspect you of a crime, having proof or probable cause that you did indeed commit that crime. Then they must swear before a judge to the credibility of that proof to get a warrant issued before they conduct the search. Tell me, when did they make it illegal to fly on an airplane? When was that outlawed? You've traveled. When were you ever handed a warrant before being searched? So how does the federal government get away with such things?"

Thomas thought, *Come on John. You know what happened on September 11, 2001.* He replied, "It's for national security."

"Oh, really? That's a good line the government uses. They've gotten real good at it too. Do you notice a trend? When we have a depression, Roosevelt slips in a 'new deal' that strips the rights of the states and the people. A national disaster strikes—terrorists blow up three of the most important buildings in America—and the federal government implements more laws that strip the people of even more of their rights. For national security! Let's see how that holds up if we come up with a plan that is constitutional.

"First the Congress passes an act that compels the states to make laws that secure our airways and airports. This is general in nature as the Constitution prescribes. Now the state governments make rules and regulations that airlines must comply with if they are to be licensed to fly in their airspace. You see, the state government can't conduct the searches themselves either because they are held to the same standard, the Fourth Amendment, as the federal government. This too is in the Constitution. That's why the state laws are directed at the airlines. The airlines, as private industry, are not subject to the Constitution. Remember that the Constitution governs only the governing body—in this case, primarily the federal government with some restrictions and rights for the state.

"So now the airlines make company policies stating that if anyone wants to fly on their private property, namely their airplanes, then customers must first go through a screening process before getting on their planes. The state, having dictated the screening procedures by their regulations, and the airlines supply the employees to conduct the searches. In this manner the Constitution is upheld and national security is maintained. So tell me again, why is the federal government searching people at the airports?"

Thomas didn't have to stop and think about the answer. It was apparent. "Because we have an abusive government," he said.

"I told you, they are masters of deception."

Thomas nodded his understanding. John continued, "I needed you to understand that so you would believe me when I say that we are not living in a democracy but a socialist nation. It's pounded in us all the time that we are a free, democratic society, but it's all a lie. Tell me, do you know when we became a communist nation?"

Thomas shook his head. "I just caught on that we are socialist, and now you tell me we're a bunch of commies!"

"Yeah," John smiled. "Welcome to the real world. Do you know the difference between socialism and communism?"

Actually, Thomas did know the difference. He had studied the former USSR when he was a freshman in high school. Phil had not been his instructor then. Thomas had found the subject interesting, so he had paid attention. He said, "Yes, I do. Basically, the ideology is the same, but in practice, communism is more a dictatorship. Also, when practiced, it has been the complete opposite of the ideology."

"Very good! Do you care to explain your last statement a little more?"

"Sure," Thomas said. "The theory is that the government owns all properties, the royalty or wealthy fade away, and the peasants are elevated to an equal class. When communism is actually applied, however, party members become the new ruling class and peasants remain peasants. It's basically a new monarchy with new titles."

Wow, John thought. *That was the briefest, most accurate description of communism in motion that he had ever heard.*

"Great! That nicely sums it up in a nutshell. Tell me, what are the trademarks of communism?"

"A highly restrictive government with a party chairman as the head honcho. They push evolution and are big-time atheists. They usually outlaw religion. Typically their products are devoid of quality. Their economy is usually repressed and… that's all I can think of off the top of my head."

"That's pretty good for coming off the top of your head. What's the press like?" asked John.

"Regulated. They believe in censorship. I believe they were called the poly-bureau. It was more for propaganda than for news."

"How about their schools?"

"State run, of course," Thomas replied. "They indoctrinate students to the party's way of thinking. I'd say it's as much a brainwashing as it is an education." The thought of Phil entered Thomas's mind for a second.

"Good. What is the most common form of birth control in a communist country?"

"Abortion."

"Okay, then," John said. "You know enough about communism that you should be able to recognize a communist when you see one. Let's go back to Roosevelt. Remember when we talked about two of his most important New Deal programs that were ruled unconstitutional by the Supreme Court?"

"Yes," replied Thomas.

"At that time, Roosevelt and his group realized that for socialism to flourish, they would have to gain control of the courts. Roosevelt's first attempt to gain control of the courts was in 1937, just after his first reelection. He asked Congress for the power to name a new justice to the Supreme Court for every member over seventy years of age who chose not to retire. In his proposal the Supreme Court would have a maximum of fifteen justices. Roosevelt's excuse was that he felt the Supreme Court needed younger, more vigorous men."

"Sounds like age discrimination," Thomas interrupted.

"Yeah. He also lied and said the Court was falling behind in its work. At that time six justices were over seventy years old, so Roosevelt's 'court-packing scheme,' as it was called, would have allowed him to gain a pro-New Deal majority on the Supreme Court."

"That was pretty brazen, wasn't it?"

"Yeah, too brazen for Congress and most of the nation. It didn't go through. It didn't matter though. Shortly after that, a Supreme Court justice retired, and Roosevelt replaced him with a staunch New Dealer. With his influence, the courts started to look more favorably upon the New Deal. Because Roosevelt was elected four times, holding office for a little over twelve years, judges naturally died off or retired. Roosevelt appointed nine of them during his reign. Naturally they were all pro-New Deal or socialist, if you will. Roosevelt also signed laws giving them more power over court procedures. This trend went on even after Roosevelt's death, with other 'Democratic' administrations.

"You know, it really goes against the grain for me to call them Democratic. It leaves a bad taste in my mouth. Anyway, sometime in the sixties, I can't remember the date or name of the act, but a law was passed expanding the power of the Supreme Court."

Thomas interrupted, "I thought the court decision we talked about said the Congress didn't have the authority to expand the powers of the Supreme Court."

"That's right, *Marbury v. Madison.* I knew you were quick. The law gave the Supreme Court the power to make case law. Now I want to show you something." John picked up the Constitution again, turned to the first page, and asked Thomas, "What does the very first paragraph of the very first section of the very first article of the Constitution say?"

"'All legislative powers herein granted shall be vested in a Congress of the United States, which shall consist of a Senate and House of Representatives.'"

When Thomas had finished reading, John asked, "Legislative powers, or more commonly known as law-making authority—how much of it was granted to Congress?"

"All of it."

"Do you see any mention of the courts having any or being given any legislative authority in this section?"

"The courts aren't mentioned at all," Thomas replied. "That law would have been unconstitutional because it violated Article One, Section One of the Constitution and because it exceeded the authority that the Congress was given."

"Correct! The courts were never to have that kind of authority," John said. "That's because the founders knew that if the courts were given this kind of authority, they would become a judicial dictatorship. They had just fought a war to throw off the bonds of one dictatorship and weren't ready, or willing, to establish a new one.

"Now on the other hand, Roosevelt and his group realized that if they were to progress and establish a socialistic government here for good, then a dictatorship would need to be established. Personally I think Roosevelt wanted to be that dictator. But there was a problem: If the president was made the dictator, the people would revolt—and there goes their scheme for socialism or communism. Like I've told you before, this group is a master of deception."

"So they used the back door," Thomas interrupted. All of it became clear. He knew what was done and how it was accomplished. "So the Democrats established the law, giving the courts the power of judicial legislation. The Congress was accustomed to socialism by this time, so they willingly established the law. The Supreme Court, being handpicked by a Democrat, was in favor of socialism. This, and the fact that they were the recipients of the power, were willing to let the law go, and—with the dictatorship going to the courts—they could make laws case by case. This was all in the name of justice, of course. The people wouldn't see it as a threat to our freedom because they couldn't pin the title on any one person, right?"

John was very impressed. This showed incredible insight on Thomas's part. His open-mindedness encouraged John to continue. This information, although quite radical to most ways of thinking, was mild compared to what he would soon discuss. John said, "You're absolutely right."

Thomas continued, "So with the establishment of a judicial dictatorship, we went from mere socialism to communism. If you had not explained it the way you did, and just told me we were a communist country, I would have told you that you were nuts and probably would have walked out on you. But now I find it hard to argue with, and it's actually quite clear. You know, John, for a communist country, we still have a lot more freedom than I would expect."

"That's because they haven't been able to apply the full stranglehold just yet. They have to take it slow, not showing too much of their hand at a time for fear that people would catch on and stop them. Remember that the Tenth Amendment gives the people a lot of power—more than they know. Although the Democratic party and those who affiliate themselves with it may have accepted Roosevelt's new definition of democracy, not everyone was a Democrat. The Republican party has been slow in coming over to their way of thinking and has kept them in check for years. Also, another group has kept them in check as well. You seem to have a pretty good grasp of the situation. You already know that Roosevelt was the assassin's hand that more or less killed the old Democratic party, but he didn't do this single-handedly. Who is the real culprit and who are the next victims?"

Thomas sat and thought for a minute. He was sure he knew the culprit that John had alluded to, but he was puzzled by the identity of the victim or victims of the next genocide. Thomas figured the Democratic party was the culprit. If that was the case, then the Republican party seemed to be the most likely victim. This seemed to be the direction John was going. With the victim of the first genocide being the original Democratic party, it just seemed natural that this would be the case.

Thomas said, "I believe the culprit is the Democratic party, and the next genocide will be the Republican party philosophy." Thomas looked at John to see if he had come close.

"You're close, but no banana," John smiled. "When you talk about this group, you generally think about Democrats, but there are some conservative Democrats out there. I told you that when this group commits genocide the next time, it's not going to be the elimination of a political system but the actual systematic execution of human lives."

John waited to see if Thomas would take another stab at it. Thomas didn't disappoint him. "I believe what you're getting at is that the killers are liberals, but I'm still not sure as to who the victims will be."

"Christians!" John said.

CHAPTER 4

A REPEAT OF HISTORY

Thomas sat back a little. He had not seen this coming. Thomas said, "John, up to now you've made sense. Your thinking has been a little unorthodox, but you've supported everything you've said with facts. But I think you're off your rocker on this one. For one thing, I don't think liberals are an organized group so much as an ideology. Do you honestly believe that Christians are in danger of being rounded up and killed by... well, by liberal-minded people?"

John gazed at Thomas with a penetrating look and firmly said, "Thomas, liberals are indeed an organized group, possibly the most organized and well-planned group society has ever produced. And I believe that within ten years, Christians will indeed be rounded up and systematically exterminated by this very group. I'm willing to bet I can present a case that will prove beyond a reasonable doubt that what I am saying is the absolute truth."

Egad! Thomas thought. *He honestly believes this! This sounds too much like a conspiracy theory. How could he have proof of such a thing?* He would hear John out, but he was going to scrutinize every word. John looked as if he expected no less. Thomas asked, "Why would liberals want to kill Christians? What would they have to gain?"

"Tom, liberals are nothing more than a hate group, just like the KKK, skinheads, Black Separatists, and Nazis. They're a hate group that puts the rest to shame, and their hatred is directed at Christians. If you have ever watched the news, you should know this. Their hate talk is politically correct. Instead of saying, 'I hate you,' they say, 'I'm offended by you. I'm offended by what you say, by what you think, by what you do, and by what you believe.' A favorite weapon of liberals is the lawsuit, and they use liberal judges who render liberal decisions. But the courts aren't their only weapon. They have a complete arsenal, deceit being the weapon of choice. To make the closest comparison of the liberal party, you have to look at the Nazi party in Germany in the 1930s and 1940s. The only difference is they are better organized and cover a greater portion of the globe. And just as the Nazis rounded up the Jews, and anyone else who opposed them, liberals will do the same thing to Christians and anyone who might try to aid them."

Thomas blurted out, "No, that could never happen here! Not here in America!"

"That's exactly what Tami said," John replied. "Tom, do you honestly think if you asked a German citizen in the mid- or even late 1930s if he believed that his country would round up over six million Jews and gas them to death, what would he have said? 'Sure, why not? It's just another form of birth control—mature abortion, if you will.' Do you honestly believe that would have been his response? Or is it more likely that he would have said, 'No, that could never happen here! Not in Germany.' Which do you think would have been the more likely answer?"

"I think he would have denied the accusation," Thomas answered, "but those were different circumstances back then."

John quickly responded, and his tone was a little condescending. "Oh, really, things were different back then? History has a way of repeating itself, my friend, and if you don't learn by it, you may die by it. Let's take another look at history, shall we? Let's look at Hitler, his beliefs, his programs and policies, and the mind-set of the German people. Let's see how similarly America and the liberal party stack up. I doubt you'll like the results.

"Remember our game. We're supposed to be detectives trying to solve a case. The hardest thing for a detective to do is come up with enough evidence to convict a suspect. Even circumstantial evidence can be used to convict a suspect as long as the preponderance of evidence can establish guilt beyond a reasonable doubt. Let's see if we have enough evidence to build a case against the liberal party. Who knows, Tom? We may save countless lives. We may even save our own lives. What do you say?"

"I'm no quitter," Thomas said. "I told you when we started this that I'd finish it. You've managed to spark my interest again. I want to see how this is going to play out."

"Great! Like I said, first we will look at Hitler and his regime."

Thomas interrupted, "I was always taught that Hitler was considered a rightist."

John grinned, "Remember, I keep telling you that these people are masters of deceit. When I say masters, I truly mean they are cunning, manipulative, and persuasive. They understand the psyche of the human mind and use it against them. For the vast majority of Americans, Hitler is synonymous with evil. Most people really didn't know Hitler's policies other than he wanted war. Who was in power in America during World War II?"

"The new socialist Democrat party run by Roosevelt."

"That's right, and after him Truman—another new era Democrat. They realized that Hitler's policies and thinking closely paralleled their own. Knowing that might leave a bad taste in most Americans' mouths, they declared him a right-wing nut. That's as far from the truth as possible. Let's examine Hitler's policies to see whether they are liberal or conservative by today's standards, shall we?"

"Okay."

"Hitler was a socialist. Nazi, short for *Nazionalsozialistische deutsche Arbeiter Portei,* is German for National Socialist German Worker's Party. Hitler and Stalin actually collaborated at the beginning of the war because they shared many of the same ideas." As he reached for a second stack of papers, John said, "This is an article written by John J. Ray. Look at some of Hitler's party programs. Read number ten aloud."

Thomas took the pages, looked them over, and began, "'The first duty of every citizen must be to work mentally or physically. The activities of the individual may not clash with the interest of the whole, but must proceed within the frame of the community and be for the general good.'" Thomas finished reading aloud, but the very next line was so belligerent that he read it as a question. "'Therefore we demand that all unearned income and all income that does not arise from work be abolished?'"

"Yep, no gifts, gratuity, or inheritance."

"This sounds more like communism."

John nodded as he took the article from Thomas. "I want you to hear his slogan." John turned some pages then read, "'*Gemeinnutz vor Eigennutz,*' which means 'common use before private use.' So tell me, who is socialistic in their party views, the liberals or conservatives?"

"The liberals."

"Okay." As John thumbed through the article again, he muttered half to himself and half to Thomas. "I have some additional notes here." When he found what he was looking for, he announced, "Here's a list of additional programs and beliefs Hitler had. He had an animal rights campaign. Is that liberal or conservative?"

"Liberal."

"He was pro-abortion, liberal or conservative?"

"Liberal."

"He was anti-Christian. Goebbels, Hitler's minister of propaganda, their version of the media, said this about Hitler, 'The Fuhrer is deeply religious, though completely anti-Christian. He views Christianity as a symptom of decay. Rightly so. It is a branch of the Jewish race... . Both have no point of contact to the animal element and thus, in the end, they will be destroyed!' Tell me, does that sound liberal or conservative?"

"Liberal."

"He signed an order for a euthanasia program. Tell me, which faction supports such ideas, the liberal or the conservative?"

"Liberal."

"Hitler was an evolutionist, liberal or conservative?"

Again, Thomas was forced to answer liberal.

"Hitler was big on gun control. Does that sound liberal or conservative to you?"

"Liberal," Thomas admitted again.

"Also, he was pro-homosexual."

"Wait a second," Thomas said. "I've always been told that he killed homosexuals in the concentration camps with the Jews. It doesn't make a bit of sense that a person who

77

was pro-homosexual would persecute them the way he did! Or was I taught a lie about that too?"

"Not all a lie. It was a half-truth."

"Which may as well be a lie," Thomas interjected.

John agreed. "It was told to serve a purpose, a selling point for the liberal agenda, and it's working well. The truth is that Hitler and his SAs, or Storm Troopers, put a lot of homosexuals in the concentration camps and identified them with a triangle on their clothes. This explains why the triangle is one of the symbols of the gay movement today. It's to remind the world of the way they have been persecuted—a sympathy factor. But they failed to tell the real reason why those homosexuals were imprisoned. And *who* was doing the imprisoning?" Thomas didn't miss John's emphasis but chose not to comment. He knew that John was about to explain.

"The real reason Hitler had those homosexuals imprisoned wasn't because of their sexual preferences," John continued. "Far from it. Most were there for political reasons, some because of the type of homosexual they were, and a few because they were sympathetic to the Jews and refused to participate in the Jewish persecution."

"Type of homosexuals?" asked Thomas.

John nodded, "If you are going to understand the threat I believe Christians are about to face, this subject is the most important and the most complex." John's stomach grumbled, so he looked at his watch. John wanted to cover this subject properly and not rush. "Since it's getting close to lunchtime, and I told Paul that we would meet him at the Rot (the nickname for the school cafeteria), we'll end here for now. We'll start back up where we left off when we get back. So, before we go, was Hitler right-wing or left-wing?" asked John.

"He was definitely a leftist," Thomas replied.

"Yep, actions speak louder than words. Modern liberals are following in Hitler's footsteps except for they're targeting Christians first instead of Jews. We'll need to look at the strategies liberals use to persecute Christianity, both the obvious and the clandestine."

"Clandestine?" asked Thomas.

"Uh-huh, attacks on the Christian faith that aren't overly apparent. They're usually disguised as some noble cause that the 'enlightened' liberals push as a better way of life." John stopped for a second to think of an example he could use to get his meaning across.

"Take for instance Washington and Oregon, both liberal states, and both passed laws making it illegal for parents to spank their children. They've taken the basic right of parents to raise and discipline their kids as they see fit. To further the liberal cause, they've used the advice of so-called child psychologists to pass these laws. Outwardly these laws don't appear to target any one group. It's just the state looking out for the well-being of our children. But as any well-versed and practicing Christian can tell you, Proverbs teaches that those who don't discipline their children, hate their children. And there is plenty of evidence of that in the world. By their passing these well-meaning laws, they have targeted Christians and hindered them from raising their kids in a godly fashion. This forces a Christian to choose between doing what is right or obeying the law. If they do what is right, they are labeled as abusive parents and criminals, putting Christianity in a bad light. By this law the liberals win in two ways: Christians who break the law make Christianity look bad, and those who obey the law run a greater risk of losing their kids to the worldly viewpoint."

"You know, John, it's obvious you're in favor of beating a kid because he makes a mistake, but I have to side with the liberals and the psychologists this time. Let's face it, psychologists are the experts. Plus my mom and dad both beat me once, and I never want to do that to my kids."

"How did your parents beat you, Tom?"

John's gaze and his question flustered Thomas. John made it sound as if his parents beat him all the time, when each had beaten him only once as far as he could remember. He didn't want John thinking his parents were some kind of monsters. Thomas felt he had great parents. He wanted to stress that those were isolated cases.

"Well, when I was about six or seven years old, I remember getting into my father's hobby cabinet. He likes to build wooden models of biplanes and boats. He caught me playing with his tools. I remember him first lecturing me about how dangerous his tools could be and how I should have respected his personal property. He used his stern voice, letting me know I had done something really wrong. He told me he was going to make sure that I remembered that lesson. He turned me around and slapped me on the butt with his hand. He struck me about three times. My mom was furious and screamed at him for hitting me. That was the last time he hit me. He grounded me a time or two, but he never hit me again." Thomas paused, expecting John to comment. John slightly nodded his head to reassure him he was listening and encouraged him to continue.

"My mom beat me once too. I remember that really well. I was ten. My mom had just bought a very expensive vase and set it on the library table in the foyer. She was just standing there admiring it when I ran inside to get something to drink. I bumped the table, and naturally the vase fell to the floor, shattering. I told her I was sorry, but it didn't matter. She picked up the candlestick that was on the table and started beating me with it. See this scar over my eye?" Thomas pointed to his left eye. "She nailed me there, and it took four stitches to close."

"She beat you on your head?"

"No, she just hit me there once. Most of the blows landed on my arms and back. My father heard my screams and pulled her off. He sent her to her room, then took me to the hospital. He asked me to tell the doctor that I had fallen from the swings. He said it was my choice, but if I told the truth, Mom would go to jail. So I told the doctor I jumped from my swing set, tripped, and hit my head on a rock. So you see, John, I can't condone beating a kid because he makes a mistake. I really don't care what the Bible says about it."

"Neither the Bible nor I condone beating your children. What your father did was controlled, thoughtful, and purposeful. What he did was legitimate. But what your mother did was criminal. That was total child abuse. That is something no one should condone."

"What's the difference?" Thomas asked. "If your mother hits you with her hand or an object, hitting is hitting, is it not?"

John realized that Thomas was getting hot, so he sat back in his chair, took a few moments, then in a very calm voice said, "Because of your experience as a child, it's clear to see why you may think so. Maybe had I had a similar experience, I might be inclined to agree with you, but I didn't. When I grew up, my mother spanked me with a wooden spoon and then my father came home and lectured me. You know something, Tom? I deserved every spanking I received. Never would I say I was abused. There's a difference between a beating and a spanking. One is a controlled, proper use of force; the other is an uncontrolled and an improper use of force. I personally can't cite the psychological difference, but I do know it exists. Find any adult you feel is well-adjusted, and I'll lay money down that his parents spanked him."

"Believe what you may, but I still don't think that hitting is the right way to discipline a child."

It was obvious Thomas was emotional about this subject and, therefore, close-minded to any idea that contradicted his beliefs. John calmly replied, "I'm not here to debate child rearing. I only used this example because it was the first thing to come to my mind to show a clandestine attack on Christianity. There are others, but we don't have the time to discuss them if we are going to meet Paul on time for lunch."

John started to pile the books into three stacks. Some of the books and papers were his. He put those in one stack, a couple of the library books he thought he still might need, and the last stack were those he felt he could put away. Thomas quickly calmed down and was clearly his old self again. Relaxed... cool. John asked if he would take the stack of books he felt he was done with and put them in their respective shelves.

As Thomas was collecting the books, he commented on a thought he had earlier. He said, "You know, John, this all sounds like a conspiracy theory." John paused, looking at him, then fished out his dictionary that he had already stowed in his backpack.

He told Thomas, "I'm going to need one of those history books you have. The one titled, *United States History Heritage of Freedom*. I need to show you something."

"What about Paul?" Thomas asked.

"This will take only a minute. I want to show you this before we put the book away."

Thomas put the books back on the table and dug out the one John had requested. John thumbed through his dictionary until he found the word—actually two words—he was looking for. Thomas placed the book in front of John, who handed him the dictionary and pointed to the words.

"Please read the definitions of conspiracy and conspire out loud."

"'Conspiracy—a plot, especially an illegal one. Conspire—to plan secretly, especially to commit an illegal act; plot. And to combine or act together.'"

While Thomas read, John looked up something in the history book. When John had found it, he said to Thomas, "Simply put, a conspiracy is when two or more people plan to do something, normally something illegal, or people combine forces or act together for a common goal. I want you to remember these definitions as we go through the rest of the day. What I'm talking about is not a conspiracy theory, it's a conspiracy, and it's a historically recorded conspiracy. I want you to read this paragraph about Roosevelt's 'advisors.'"

Thomas read, "'The "Brain Trust." In the proposals that FDR made to Congress during the "Hundred Days," as well as in many of his later programs, he followed the advice of a group of close advisors, mostly college professors, who came to be known as the "Brain Trust." They urged the adoption of the untried and unproven economic theories of John Maynard Keynes. Keynes was a British left-wing economic theoretician who advocated central planning and massive economic and social intervention on the part of government.'"

"That's good," John interrupted. "Although the public was aware of the 'Brain Trust,' it in no way diminishes the fact that this group and FDR conspired to initiate programs that violated the Constitution, and the Constitution is the law of the land, thus a conspiracy. Just because these policies and actions were taken for economic recovery, don't think there weren't ulterior political and sociological motivations involved. As we discussed earlier, FDR's Agricultural Adjustment Act and the National Recovery Act were not in the best interest of the people, as claimed, but designed to slow recovery so as to establish socialism as the Democratic platform. It was mostly for the liberal agenda.

"When we come back from lunch, we'll see how Hitler did the same thing. Publicly he announced one reason for an action, but privately he was motivated by another. Remember actions speak louder than words, and history has a way of revealing things that are not readily apparent at the time."

"That might have been a conspiracy back then, but the 'Brain Trust' is long gone. Who are the conspirators now?"

"How do you know the 'Brain Trust' is long gone? Do you honestly believe that a group of college professors who got that taste of power just faded away?"

Thomas answered John's question with a question. "What? You think they started a secret society?"

"Is that totally impossible?"

"Well no, but it sounds kind of nutty."

"As I said earlier, actions speak louder than words. I asked you to keep in mind the definition of conspire. Especially keep in mind the second definition—to combine efforts and act together for a common goal. While we build a case against the liberal party, let's see if there is a common front. I think when you look at the big picture, you'll find it obvious. Then I want you to explain one thing to me. How could such an enormous undertaking be accomplished without guidance? I have another question for you. Where did you get the idea that a conspiracy theory is nutty?"

Thomas thought about it and said, "I don't know. Everyone knows that conspiracy theories are mostly from people with hyperactive imaginations."

"You get that pretty much from the media, don't you?"

Thomas pondered the thought before answering. "Yeah, that's usually where we hear about most conspiracies."

"Would you classify the media as liberal or conservative?" John asked.

"For the most part, it's liberal. Do you think they are part of this conspiracy?"

"We'll see. Just think about this. If you had a multitude of resources and were conspiring to change a culture and didn't want the opposition to unravel that conspiracy, wouldn't it be nice to convince society that 'conspiracy theories' are for nut cases and not to be taken seriously?"

"That sounds like a pretty elaborate scheme to me."

"It is!" John agreed. "I've told you that liberals are masters of deception—and they have had over seventy years to get their pawns in place."

"Pawns?"

"Like in chess, liberals use people like they are expendable. After lunch we'll look at the resources and tactics that liberals use to bully their views on the people. Here..." John handed Thomas the history book and asked him to put away the ones he had been given. While Thomas did that, John jotted down some notes. He also placed a note on top of the remaining library books he thought he might need, asking that they be left there until they returned. The books he owned he put in his pack and was ready to go by the time Thomas returned.

As they departed Corette Library, Thomas held the door open for John and asked, "My mom is an adamant Democrat. Does this mean that she is a co-conspirator?"

Usually John's strides were like Paul Bunyon's, but as he talked, that purposeful stride tapered off. John slowed his gait to more of a saunter as they walked to the student hall. John had felt Thomas was a little more defensive than he expected while talking about conspiracies. He assumed

85

Thomas was still a little bit rattled about their talk on discipline. Now he felt that the undercurrent of hostility was probably in defense of his mother. John had met Thomas's parents earlier that year when they came to visit him and learned she was a devout Catholic as well.

"Tell me, Tom, does your mother believe in abortion?"

"No."

"Does she believe in gay marriages?"

"She doesn't even believe that gays should be allowed any kind of partner benefits, much less marriage."

"Does she support our troops in Iraq?"

"Yes, she supports our troops over there, but I know she doesn't approve of this war."

"The liberal Democratic party is responsible for pushing pro-abortion bills and laws on this country. It has also firmly supported the gay movement. The liberal Democratic party has cut the budget of the armed forces and prevented our soldiers, the best in the world, from getting the type of pay and benefits they so rightly deserve. How can your mother claim to disapprove of abortion and gay marriage, and claim to support our troops, and say she is a Democrat?"

Thomas fell silent as he thought of an appropriate answer.

John, however, broke the silence first. "I'll tell you how. Let me know if I am wrong. It's because her father was a Democrat, her mother was a Democrat, her grandfather was a Democrat, her grandmother was a Democrat, and most likely her great-grandparents were Democrats. She comes from a family of Democrats, and Democrats vote Democratic.

"The reason political parties evolved was so that persons with 'common' beliefs could stand together and have strength in numbers to support their ideas. It also gave other people with similar thoughts a political icon to identify with and thus join the cause. The key to political parties is supposed to be support of like-minded thinking.

"The problem is people like to take on labels. We label ourselves by our religion, by our work, by our party, by the type of sports we like. We love our labels. You know, basically that's all psychology really is. It's observing human behavior and giving labels to those behaviors. Once we take on a label, we pretty much do what is expected of that label.

"This fits the case of calling oneself a Democrat. The ideas that the party leaders adopt don't truly matter. If the Democrats do it, then it's the Democratic thing to do. Support your party! There comes a time when the label overrides free will and independent thought. Just do as the party says. It's this human trait that FDR and his cronies depended on when they chose to run under the old Democratic party and not the socialist party that was already in place. A good number of Americans already labeled themselves Democrats. It made their jobs easier.

"No, your mother is not a conspirator. Neither is the vast majority of the people who label themselves Democrats. They're just followers. Really, percentage-wise, you don't need a whole lot of conspirators. They do have to be in key positions, but you don't need many of them."

"How is that?"

"Let's use the Senate as an example. I'm sure there are some major liberal conspirators there. Let's say out of the forty-five or so members of the Democratic party, only seven of those members are actually conspirators—those who know all the fine points of the final purpose of the plot. One drafts a bill that will forward their cause. He is immediately supported by two of the co-conspirators while the other four hang back. The original three approach a group of fellow Democrats. In that group is one of their members.

The original three share their proposals with the group. If there seems to be any hesitation in the group, the plant starts singing its praises of how Democratic it is, how brilliant it is. The hesitation falters, and the four conspirators bring peer pressure to bear until there is agreement. This cycle repeats itself until all that is needed is peer pressure. They sing out, 'Be a Democrat, support a Democrat,' and like puppets, the masses of Democrats join the choir."

"Does this only happen in the political arena?" Thomas asked.

John shook his head no and said, "I'm going to go out on a limb here. Although I don't have any direct proof, I'll bet it's safe to guess that Ted Turner is most likely part of the inner circle in the liberal party. He is an admitted Christian hater. Do you think any of the employees at CNN would dare air a story that showed Christians in a good light? I don't think so—not if they want to keep their jobs. People are easily led or misled as the case might be. Let's just call the inner circle the 'Brain Trust' for now as a reference. The Brain Trust doesn't have to be enormous; it just has to hold key positions in society. Those positions will be in politics, the courts, the unions, the media, the boards of education, and as leaders in psychology."

"Why those places?"

"First, that's where the power is. Second, that's the way Hitler did it."

CHAPTER 5

LUNCH

They had reached the student hall and headed to the cafeteria on the second floor. Not too many students had arrived this early in the lunch period. They quickly spotted Paul sitting toward the back and walked over. It looked as if he hadn't touched his food yet. John greeted him first as he slung his backpack on the ground and took the seat opposite of him.

"Hey, dude, you're early," John smiled.

"No, you're late!" Paul shot his comeback.

"That's because I had a hard time convincing Tom to come here. He wanted to eat at the Staggering Ox. I told him you had planned to meet us here. He said that was your problem."

Paul looked at his chili-mac and said, "I think he's right."

"That's not what I said," Thomas interjected. "I said we should get some real food at the Ox, then come back here, and eat it in front of you."

"Your such a true freind." Paul replied.

Actually the school cafeteria put out a pretty good product. At the beginning of the year the students were more than willing to eat there, but the cafeteria food had lost its appeal by the beginning of March. Summer break would be a welcomed relief. Still, it was the most economical place to eat in town.

"Have you been here long?" John asked.

"I just started to sit down when you two came through the door," Paul said.

"Good, we'll be back in a minute to join you," said John.

Both headed toward the cafeteria line. Thomas opted for the burger and fries. John chose the chicken salad. Paul's reaction to the main course, a chili-mac, solidified their thoughts that it was definitely not an option. Soon they were back at the table, talking about the night's outing. John had purposely kept the topic away from their investigation. Thomas seemed a little tense, and John wanted to give him a chance to wind down.

The gang had planned on seeing *Hidalgo* at the theater since it started in March. About fourteen of them wanted to meet for dinner and a movie. Because of their hectic schedules, however, coordinating a time when everyone could get together was a nightmare. This was the last week of the engagement. The show started at 7:15 P.M. Anyone who wanted to eat dinner before the movie would meet at St. Charles Hall at 5:30 P.M.

One question needed to be answered: Where do we eat? The guys had narrowed the choices down to three places: Applebees, McKenzie River Pizza, or the Brewhouse. The guys figured the girls would decide. One of the guys would ask, "Where does everyone want to eat?" The guys already knew the consensus would be that it really didn't matter. Then the guy who asked the question would suggest the three restaurants. Everyone would agree that they were good choices, and then the process of elimination began.

One of the guys would ask about the first restaurant to see what kind of response the gals would give. If they responded, "I'm not sure," then they moved to the next selection until everyone, or at least a majority of the girls, seemed excited about the choice. That would be where they would eat that night.

Right now the guys were talking movies. Paul said, "I like the previews where the guy rides his horse and that wall of sand comes at him. I couldn't imagine what that would be like in real life."

"I can," Thomas said. "When I was young, my parents had taken us to Las Vegas for vacation. We were just sitting around the hotel room with the door open. My sister and I were playing on the balcony when this great big wall of sand suddenly started moving toward us. We told our father to come quick and look at the funny clouds. My sister and I didn't know what it was, but my dad did. He shuffled us into the room and shut the door just as the storm hit the hotel. My mom was nervous, but Kattie and I were excited and watched it through the window. It didn't last long, at least not long enough for me and Kattie. I rememeber after it ended, Kattie and I went to the swimming pool. There was sand everywhere—even at the bottom of the pool. We wanted to swim in the worst way, but Mom wouldn't let us."

"Sounds cool," Paul said. "What hotel were you staying in?"

"I don't remember the name of it. It wasn't one of the big ones. It was just a small, two-level one."

"It sounds like The Sands to me," John said.

Both Thomas and Paul scrunched their eyes and shook their heads. Paul said, "Oh, that was horrible."

Thomas continued with the conversation and said, "Do you know what movie I'm looking forward to seeing? It's *Troy*. I think it comes out in June."

"Yeah, that looks like it's going to be a great one," Paul said. "I like that one scene in the previews where they show the sea filled with ships ready to invade."

"Isn't it cool what they can do with computer graphics nowadays?" John said. "They make movies so much more lifelike."

"I know," Thomas said. "Look at *Lord of the Rings* and what they did with Gollum. He looked so real it was scary."

Paul said, "Yeah, just goes to show you, you can't even trust a picture nowadays."

John said, "You know, a page in one of my Calvin and Hobbs books makes that very point. Calvin takes a picture of himself in his room and tells Hobbs how pictures are misleading. For the picture he combs his hair and cleans only half of his room. He tells Hobbs, 'See, this picture captures my room as being clean and me as a neat child. It fails to show the rest of the story and what I'm like after the photo is taken.' Then Calvin messes his hair again. But it's a wonderful illustration of how a picture can be used to deceive."

"True," Thomas said. "When movie directors can make you believe we've brought dinosaurs back to life, there's no telling what they can fabricate."

"You know what I think would be fun?" As John spoke he glanced at Paul, who seemed to be looking more past him than at him. "Being an extra in a movie like *Lord of the...*"

Before he could finish his sentence, two hands came from behind to cover his eyes. A sweet voice softly said in his ear, "Guess who?"

John grinned while he questioned this soft-spoken newcomer. "Tell me, do you have a heart full of love and a spirit as kind as your face is beautiful?"

Hesitantly, the soft voice replied, "I don't know about all of that." The soft, silky hands still covered John's eyes.

"Are you as modest as you are wonderfully brilliant?" John asked.

Embarrassed by the question, the woman with the soft voice said, "I don't know."

"Mom!" John said. "What are you doing here?"

John quickly turned and gave a mock look of surprise to see Rebecca standing there. Rebecca played along and lightly slapped John on the shoulder, pretending to be offended. "Thanks a lot."

"Well, if I had added attractive, vivacious, and the desire of every young man's heart, I would have known it was you," John said.

Tami Jankins said, "Oh, please! I didn't know I was going to have to bring my waders to the lunchroom." She moved to a seat between Thomas and John. Rebecca said, "I love you too, girlfriend." She took a seat from the table next to theirs and moved it next to John. Dori Garris was hungry so she decided to stand behind Rebecca until she sat down with a plate of food. Dori wasn't a big eater. She hadn't eaten that morning and had forgotten to eat the night before because of her studies. Being in the cafeteria made her realize she was famished.

"Hi, guys," the girls greeted. Thomas looked upon Dori approvingly. There weren't too many men who didn't. Dori wore a pink, low-cut knit shirt. Her stylish, low rider jeans accented her figure. She had naturally wavy, dark brown bordering on black hair. Her deep blue eyes, wide and lively, attracted attention. She possessed a smooth complexion and a warm, inviting smile. She stood at about five feet seven with a super body, a woman well endowed. Simply put, she was gorgeous. And men let her know it. It was not uncommon for a carload of guys to yell out as they drove by or for strangers to walk up and ask her out. She said yes more times than not.

For the most part their group went out as just that, a group. In the two years that these friends had been doing things together only John and Rebecca had become serious about each other. The others had contemplated the possibility of a relationship with each other, but things never seemed to work out.

Thomas had taken Dori out twice with romance on his mind. But at the end of each date, Dori thanked him for a nice evening and turned in without so much as a kiss goodnight. Frustrated at first, Thomas found out that Sam and Paul had dated her as well and received the same treatment. Most of the guys on campus labeled her as a tease. Dori knew this and didn't really care. She figured those who labeled her did so because they were after only one thing. And she was looking for something more.

A small-town girl from North Dakota, Dori loved to ski. Her favorite place was Big Mountain, a fairly popular ski resort in the northwest part of Montana near Whitefish. She had skied Aspen, Vail, and Breckenridge in Colorado and Tahoe in Nevada, but still her favorite was Big Mountain. It was a major contributing factor why she had chosen Carroll College for her higher education, along with the fact that its nursing school program had a good reputation. Most important, Big Mountain was only four hours away. Her friends didn't understand why she didn't go pro or join the Olympics or something. She always told them that she skied for her own satisfaction and wasn't interested in competing. Most of the guys thought it was a waste of talent, but they never pressured her into competing.

While Thomas looked her over, he thought that he should pursue another chance with her. Although Thomas would openly admit that he was too young for marriage, he didn't see anything wrong with casual courtship. Watching Dori eye Paul, however, quickly changed Thomas's mind. *What a mixed up group of friends,* Thomas thought. He was attracted to Dori, but she was obviously interested in Paul. Paul had the hots for Tami. She had the hots for the assistant manager at the local sandwich shop, and the assistant manager had the hots for himself. The only ones who seemed to have it right were John and Rebecca.

Rebecca was the shortest of the girls, standing only five feet one, but she was every bit as attractive as her two friends. Rebecca's grandparents had immigrated from Mexico. Her grandfather, a machinist, got a job with a mining company in Anaconda, Montana. Because of complications at birth, Rebecca's grandmother was able to have only one child, Rebecca's mother, Rosa. Rosa grew up in Anaconda and married James Wright who, with his father, owned and ran a local business.

You could see Rebecca's Hispanic heritage. She had dark brown hair with red highlights, brown eyes, and a slightly darker complexion than her friends. Her petite but well-proportioned frame attracted the attention of men. Her eyes and her smile radiated a friendly warmth. You could see the intelligence behind her eyes. There was little wonder why John had snagged her, although it had looked like John and Tami were going to be an item when the group first started doing things together.

Tami, the beautiful blonde of the three, liked to wear her hair short, usually off her shoulders. Like Dori, she had deep, brilliant blue eyes. Her five-feet six-inch frame was athletic and toned. Unlike the other two, however, she had a more reserved personality and wasn't so free with her smile. When she met someone new, she looked at them as if analyzing them. But once she got to know a person, she was fun loving and quite caring. Like Thomas, she was from Colorado. Instead of Littleton, however, she came from the eastern part of the Denver metropolitan area called Aurora.

She chose Carroll College because she had an aunt and an uncle living in Helena. Actually her uncle lived in East Helena, but that was close enough. The weird thing was that her aunt and her husband were from her mother's side and her uncle and his family were from her father's side. Tami liked it because it was away from Mom and Dad so she could gain her independence yet close enough to family just in case.

These students had become a group right there in the cafeteria. The year before, John, Paul, and Sam were sophomores and Tami, Rebecca, and Dori were freshmen. While standing in the cafeteria line, John and Sam had debated theology. They argued about the identity of Behemoth in the Book of Job. After getting nowhere with John, Sam turned to the next person in line, who happened to be Rebecca, and said, "Will you tell my friend here that the Behemoth mentioned in Job was a hippopotamus?"

"No," John said, "if anything it was a crocodile."

Rebecca calmly replied, "You're both wrong. It's a dinosaur."

The guys just looked at her so Tami said, "She's right."

"Why is she right?" Sam asked.

Tami gave Sam a mischievous smile. "Because she's a woman!" she bantered. Needless to say, the debate started again, and the guys asked the girls to join them. After lunch the guys asked if the girls would like to meet them at the local bar for some pool. The girls accepted, and soon they became the gang. Other friends joined them from time to time, but the gang was always the six of them.

At first Tami gravitated toward John when the group got together. John never seemed to mind, although he always kept it casual, probably because he liked being around Rebecca and Dori as well. Then Tami started to date one of the football team's star jocks and didn't hang around the group as much. That's when John and Rebecca grew closer. By the time Tami dropped her new boyfriend, John and Rebecca had started to date. Before the school year ended, they were a couple. Sam always thought Tami had started to date the football jock to force John's hand to have him commit, but it backfired on her. John didn't see it that way. They were friends then and are still friends now. Rebecca and Tami had no animosity between them.

Paul was a Helena born and raised cowboy like Sam. A tall six feet two, Sam had the stocky build of a steer wrestler, a feat which he did. More trim and measuring six feet tall, Paul had well-defined muscles. Until Thomas came on board, he was considered the pretty boy of the bunch with sandy blonde hair, blue-gray eyes, and a wannabe mustache. Paul had dated Dori a couple of times and liked her. A true gentleman, Paul had always treated her like a lady. It didn't bother him one bit that she had never kissed him goodnight. He assumed it was because she was a lady.

He shied away from her because he felt he wouldn't be able to trust her. Too willing to date a complete unknown, Dori tended to go out with one guy one night and another the next. Rebecca had asked her about it one day. She said naively, "How else do you get to know people?" Rebecca had warned her that that was a dangerous way to get to know people. Dori informed her she needed to have more faith in people.

After two years of going places with the gang, Paul felt that it was time to start a real relationship with Tami. She was fun-loving and at times even the life of the group. Tami was the only one who didn't drink liquor, but when the gang went places for entertainment, she was the least inhibited. She was always the first on the dance floor, the liveliest at the bowling alley, and the first to try something new. Paul liked that.

There was only one problem. Tami wanted to keep their relationship as friends. She told him she had someone else on her mind, and to start a relationship with him would be phony. She had dated the assistant manager at the Staggering Ox, a local sandwich shop that cooked its buns in cans, giving them a peculiar shape.

Paul didn't like the guy, but for that matter, none of the guys liked him. They had walked into the shop on a number of occasions and each time found him hitting on some new pretty young thing. Actually that was his pickup line, "Aren't you a pretty young thing," and it worked! Then he lavished the girl with compliments. The guy was incredibly shallow. Whatever Tami saw in him was beyond them. Paul kept hoping she would come to her senses before he hurt her.

"You guys look like you're about finished," Rebecca said. "If we grab a bite, will you hang around, or do you need to get back to your studies?"

"Go ahead and get something to eat," John said. "We can sit with you."

The girls proceeded to get their lunches. While the ladies were in line Paul asked John, "When are you going to ask her to marry you?"

Thomas chimed in, "Yeah, the school year is almost over, and I have to go back to Littleton on summer break. My father has a good-paying summer job lined up for me, so it's going to be hard for me to be your best man if you plan a summer wedding."

"You'd be his best man?" Paul complained. "No way, runt! You're looking at the best man, and I don't see a mirror between you and me. You can be the ring bearer."

"What makes you two so sure I plan to marry her?"

Both Paul and Thomas said at the same time, "Oh, please!"

Paul continued, "You're so obviously crazy about her, a blind man could see it. She's no less crazy about you. The only real question is why aren't you married yet?"

"Yeah, so when are you going to ask her?" Thomas said.

"I'll tell you what," John said, "you two will be the second ones to know, maybe even the day after I ask Rebecca, but she will be the first." John had planned to propose to Rebecca during Christmas break and have the wedding the last week of school. He intended to make his brother, Zeke, his best man. Zeke should have been back from Iraq by then, but his plans had changed.

The girls returned to the table. Dori took a seat between Paul and Rebecca. Paul asked, "How's your day going?"

Dori smiled and said, "Pretty good. I was studying my biology. What were you guys talking about when we got here?"

"Movies," Thomas said.

"I can't wait to see *Hidalgo*," Dori said. "I love horses."

Rebecca and Tami took their seats, and Tami said, "Yeah, and Viggo Mortensen isn't bad to look at either."

"No, he's not," Dori said. "He needs to make a movie where he wears tights."

"What, like Robin Hood?" Thomas said.

"Men in tights," John and Paul joined in.

Thomas continued, "I don't think so. He's definitely the Aragorn type."

Paul said, "John wants to be an extra in a movie."

"Yeah, I think it would be a kick to be in a picture like *Lord of the Rings* or *Gladiator.*"

"You know what movie I would have liked to have been an extra in?" Rebecca asked. "*A Knight's Tale.* I would have loved to have worn some of those dresses seen at the ball scenes."

The conversation quickly turned to what fashions the girls would want to wear from the various movies they had seen. While the conversation went on, Thomas thought about his discussion with John. The topic of disciplining kids poked its way to the forefront of his mind. John had challenged him to find well-adjusted adults and ask them if they were spanked as children. Rebecca was the most well-adjusted person Thomas had ever met. He admired her quiet self-assurance and confidence. She was good humored, intelligent, and considerate without a sign of conceit. She was what he called genuine. There was no pretense about her.

Thomas decided this would be a good time to ask her if she had ever been spanked as a child. The fact that John would hear her answer was even better. During the next lull in the conversation, Thomas asked Rebecca, "Hey, Rebecca, I'm curious. This is from a conversation John and I had earlier. Were you ever spanked as a child?"

John raised an eyebrow, and Rebecca gave Thomas a funny look. Although nobody noticed it, Dori turned a little ashen when she heard the question. Rebecca replied, "Well, yeah. When I needed it, my father spanked me."

Thomas looked surprised. Actually he wore a blank expression.

"My mother did the spankings at my house," Paul chimed in. "My father gave the talking to's. Mom used a wooden spoon. When we misbehaved, my mom pulled out a wooden spoon and said, 'Don't make me use my favorite spoon on you!' Heck! My mom must have broken a favorite wooden spoon on my butt at least once a week! I think my father had stock in the lumberyard."

"My father was smarter," Tami added. "He whittled a paddle from a stick. We kids used to wish that thing would break."

"Did you get spanked often as a kid?" Paul asked her.

"Me?" Tami asked. "I was a perfect angel. I never got spanked. Well," she said wolfishly, "almost never."

"I know John here gets spanked," Rebecca smiled. "He, his mom, and I were in the kitchen before Thanksgiving dinner. Ruth was talking about some of her friends getting together and playing cards. Brain child here called them 'broads.' Ruth picked up a wooden spoon, came up behind him, smacked him across the backside, and said, 'Don't you ever let me hear you degrade women like that again. I taught you better respect than that.' John put his head down like a child and said, 'Yes, ma'am.'"

Practically everyone laughed at the story. Tami commented, "Oh, I like that woman." Only Thomas sat in stunned disbelief. Even Dori had loosened up. She even looked relieved.

For the longest time Dori felt she had been living with a dark secret—one that was too horrible and embarrassing to share. Because her father had spanked her and her siblings as kids, she had always felt he was a child abuser—a person with a sick mind who needed counseling. At least that's what her middle and high school counselor would have said. Dori loved her father very much and never wanted to expose what the counselor would call his "brutality" to the public.

But now her best friends talked openly and approvingly of the way their parents had disciplined them. She felt as if a giant anvil had been lifted off her chest. Something inside her wanted confirmation that her father wasn't an abuser. So she volunteered her experience as a child.

"When we got into trouble, my father used a belt on us. Do you think using a belt is abusive?"

"Where did he hit you?" Rebecca asked.

"Only on the buttocks."

"How many times would he strike you there?"

"Only twice, you could count on it. They usually sounded worse than they felt. The belt snapped each time it struck."

"I don't think I'd ever use a belt but, no, that definitely wasn't abuse," Rebecca concluded.

Dori beamed at her comment. She had the urge to phone home and tell her father she loved him.

Thomas couldn't handle it any longer. He confronted Rebecca, "How can you sit there and condone someone beating you? It's barbaric!" The table became quiet.

Rebecca stared at Thomas for several moments then said, "Far from it. Actually discipline is just the complete opposite when done correctly." Then Rebecca said something that baffled Thomas. It wasn't only her words but the way she spoke them—matter of factually and not even in the form of a question. "You were beaten as a child." All eyes turned to Rebecca, then to Thomas. He felt an overwhelming desire to escape and to defend his parents.

"I've been spanked only twice in my life. My father spanked me on the butt once."

"And the second time?" Rebecca inquired.

"My mom spanked me once too," Thomas replied.

Rebecca leaned forward and questioned, "Spanked?" Her obvious skepticism made Thomas more uncomfortable than ever. Why had he broached the subject? He knew why. He was sure everyone would be appalled by the concept of spanking a child for the sake of discipline. John would learn a lesson himself today. Instead Thomas had his head in a noose. Rebecca knew.

Thomas glared at John as if to accuse him of sharing his secret. But that could not be. He had been with John the entire time. Thomas returned Rebecca's penetrating gaze. *Well,* he thought, *just go ahead and tell her the truth. It wasn't all that bad. My mother had beaten me only once. Everyone has admitted to being beaten several times. How could what had happened to me be any different?*

Thomas finally admitted, "My mother beat me with a candlestick."

With the exception of John, who already knew it, everyone at the table gasped. Their reaction baffled Thomas. When they talked about their own beatings, they had laughed.

"Where did she beat you?" asked Rebecca.

"Well, mostly on my arms."

"That was because you were warding off blows. Where did she strike you when you weren't protecting yourself?"

"On the back." Thomas looked at John, who met his gaze and then glanced at the scar over his left eye. Thomas continued, "She also gave me the scar over my eye."

"Oh, how horrible!" Dori exclaimed.

At the same time Paul, of all people, said, "That's not right."

Tami shook her head with a sympathetic look. Their reactions confused Thomas. Rebecca said, "Tom, what your mother did was absolutely wrong. Although you probably don't understand this, there is a difference between punishment and brutality."

Thomas was no longer adamant about his view on spanking. He simply asked, "How are they different?"

Rebecca's reply almost echoed what John had said earlier. "A beating is an uncontrolled outpouring of rage. A spanking is a deliberate, decisive, controlled act. A beating is a violent act where blows are delivered anywhere on the body. Spankings are traditionally applied to the buttocks or the back of the hand and are designed to promote learning right and wrong. Beatings are the venting of one's anger or aggression. They are usually masked as discipline but don't achieve the same effect. Instead of being a stimulus for learning, they produce psychological damage." Rebecca paused to see if Thomas wanted to comment. He merely stared at her, waiting for her conclusion.

"Spanking accomplishes three things. First, it gets your children's attention. Second, pain stimulates memory retention, and third, it leaves no doubt that the action leading to the spanking was wrong. Of course spanking shouldn't be a parent's first line of discipline. A parent should use positive reinforcement, praising their children when they do right. A child should first be disciplined with verbal commands and tutoring before a spanking. Many child psychologists condone spanking as an essential part of child rearing."

John cut in then. "Aside from all of that psychology stuff, I look at the world around me for real-life situations. My neighbor back home in Butte raised her kids with a liberal attitude. 'Don't interfere with your kid's development. Don't restrain them with old-fashioned standards of conduct. Let them find their individuality.' She didn't believe in spankings. One of her sons is in prison. The other has a nowhere job that he uses to keep him swimming in alcohol. One of her daughters was so heavily into drugs, that even now, after drying out, she suffers from paranoid delusions. Her youngest daughter can't stay in a marriage.

By the way, my neighbor is divorced too. So tell me, Tom, which is more abusive—allowing your kids to ruin their lives or training your kids to be healthy, productive adults? Which is the abuse?"

"That's just one case," Thomas replied.

Rebecca responded, "Statistically adults who didn't have proper discipline are more likely to have social disorders than those who did."

John said, "Liberals have a reverse Machiavellian philosophy. Niccolo Machiavelli's famous quote was 'The end justifies the means.' This meant no matter how unscrupulous the means by which you achieved a goal, as long as the end product resulted in the good of all, it was okay. Most of society considers that outrageous and evil. The liberal philosophy is 'the means justifies the end.' That is, no matter how terrible things wind up, as long as they meant well, it's OK. Which philosophy do you believe is the more evil?"

Paul said, "The road to hell is paved with good intentions, as the old adage goes."

Thomas wasn't sure what to say, but it didn't matter. John ended the situation by telling everyone that Thomas and he had better get back to the library if they were going to make it to dinner and the movie on time.

As they got up the girls looked sympathetically toward Thomas. Paul even patted Thomas on the shoulder in a gesture of sympathy. Paul never showed sympathy to anyone! The two exited the student center and didn't talk much on their way to the library. Thomas pondered the lunch conversation. Although not totally convinced that spanking a child was a good thing, he was not going to be so closed-minded to it either.

CHAPTER 6

HISTORY REPEATS ITSELF— A CLOSER LOOK

When John and Thomas reached their table, they found the books they had left there untouched. They sat down, and John removed his books, articles, and notes from his backpack. He looked at the notes he had written before going to lunch and said, "OK, a quick review. We established that this nation was founded on the principle of Christianity. We went over how the old Democratic party was murdered, and how Roosevelt established a new 'Democratic' party philosophy, which was socialism, or closer to the truth, communism. By the way, don't worry about labels like socialism, communism, or fascism. In reality they are the same thing, just with varying degrees of control over the people."

"A rose is but a rose by any other name," Thomas said.

"Correct, and these are just as thorny. I also accused the liberal movement of having the identical agenda as the old Nazi Germany Third Reich except that liberals are targeting Christians first instead of Jews. I also stated my belief that they will, within ten years, start to execute Christians like the Nazis executed the Jews. We went over a list of Hitler's programs and correlated those with the liberal agenda.

"We had begun to talk about one of the deceitful strategies of the liberal party, the gay movement, and I started to discuss how Hitler used homosexuality for his cause. The last question you asked was the differences in homosexual types, and it was a very important question. First, however, I want to cover the political engines that Hitler used to get a nation to hate and destroy a religious group. The first thing Hitler did was gain control over the courts. He put in judges who were sympathetic to, or in total agreement with, his cause the same way Franklin Roosevelt did. Just like the liberal Democratic party does today. Remember recently how President Bush tried to nominate two judges—Judge Miguel Estrada and Judge Priscilla Owen? Do you recall how hard the Democrats fought to keep them out of that position? Judge Estrada was Hispanic, and Judge Owen was a woman. Both had great records and good reputations within their communities. Don't the Democrats claim they are for the advancement of minorities and women? So why did they fight so hard to keep them out of office?"

"Because they were conservatives."

"That's right. It doesn't matter if the potential judge is highly qualified. The key people ask: Is that person a liberal, and will he or she advance the liberal cause? Remember when I said earlier that one of the liberal's favorite weapons was the courtroom?"

Thomas thought back to when John had revealed that the murderers in this game were the liberals. John had mentioned that the courts were one of their favorite weapons but had moved on to talk about deceit. Thomas nodded and said, "I remember."

"They use the terrorist group, the ACLU, as their trigger man," said John.

108

Thomas smiled at his choice of words. It was obvious what John thought of the ACLU. Although he shared the sentiment, he said, "I don't think too many people would classify the ACLU as terrorist."

John picked up the Constitution again and turned to the back where he had typed additional notes, then acknowledged Thomas, saying, "You're more than likely right. Most Americans think terrorists are Arabs with dynamite strapped to them, but would you like to hear the definition that the government gives to terrorists? This is a copy from a federal manual. I got this from a Fed friend of mine who attends my church. Listen to this. 'Terrorism is the calculated use of force, violence, or threat of violence against persons or property to achieve a political or religious goal. These goals are achieved through intimidation, coercion, fear, or by seeking ransom. Terrorism is directed against governments, businesses, communities, and individuals. It may be done to retaliate for perceived injustices; to cause a confrontation between parties; to improve a bargaining position; or to demonstrate strength, commitment, and resolve.'

"The ACLU has gone hog wild with the number of lawsuits they have filed. And for what purpose? To achieve a political goal at the very least. It may achieve religious goals as well, as we may find out later in our investigation. But it is definitely for political goals. By using the so-called 'separation of church and state' as a means of political activism, they have stripped America of many of our time-honored traditions and heritage. Examples include removing the Ten Commandments from our courthouses or public buildings, removing prayer from school, and making it a crime to practice our religion at the workplace. These examples infringe on our First Amendment rights that say 'or prohibiting the free exercise thereof.'

"Through their lawsuits they have made Christmas an unlawful practice, forcing merchants to use the phrase, 'happy holidays' for fear of offending someone. What holidays could they possibly be talking about? There are only two that time of year. Both are religious and pay tribute to the one true God. What do they fear? A lawsuit. You see, the courts are their weapon. If any group does not conform to their political or religious viewpoint, they sue them or threaten to sue them."

John paused to see if Thomas wanted to comment. Thomas realized that John had more to say, so he just nodded.

"A lawsuit is the greatest form of intimidation," John continued. "It is a 'legal' way to strip one of money and property and force one to act against his own free will. What difference does it make if a terrorist blows up your house or takes it away from you in a lawsuit? In both ways you are deprived of your property. What difference does it make if a terrorist shoots you or has a court strip you of your dignity and beliefs, leaving you as powerless as a puppet? People bob their heads yes to the every whim of the terrorist for fear of imprisonment. That is slavery. As Patrick Henry said, 'Give me liberty or give me death.' For many of us, slavery is a fate worse than death.

"So the way that the ACLU uses the courts amounts to nothing more than terrorism. The courts are no longer a vessel of justice but an instrument of intimidation and extortion. If the Arabs had half a brain, they would dump all their guns and bombs and sue America in an international court. We would be on our knees in a heartbeat, doing anything they liked."

"I've never thought of it that way before," Thomas said.

"That's because we're trained to follow the leader and never to think outside of the box. Right now the liberals are usurping the lead—and where they are leading us is frightening. No decent human being should want to go."

Thomas nodded as he thought about what John had just said.

"You know that the federal government subsidizes the ACLU," John said. "I guess that makes us a terrorist nation."

"Does that mean we declared war on ourselves?"

John and he both laughed. Thomas had a knack for using humor to loosen up a serious moment.

"Let's get back to our investigation," John said. "The next political engine Hitler used was the media. Tell me, is today's mainstream media liberal or conservative?"

"We definitely have a liberal press corps."

"Yeah, it's obvious. But I always thought the press was supposed to be unbiased, dealing in facts. You know what truly gets me? If the government passed a law to censor the press, people would scream. Yet the media practices censorship on a routine basis, and no one says a word. What difference does it make if the government or the press censors a story? In either case, the people are denied the facts to make an informed decision. In either case, the people are manipulated into thinking what the censor wants them to think. I'd rather have the government do the censoring. Then you know you're being lied to and can question their views.

"The third major political engine Hitler used was the education system. He achieved the most damage and greatest control when his group infiltrated the *Wandervogel,* something like the German boy scouts. We'll get into that shortly. You went to public school. Did they teach you about homosexuality?"

"They call it diversity training. They teach that nothing is wrong with having a different type of lifestyle."

"Uh-huh, right! Unless you want to be a Christian. Let's look at the side of homosexuality your teachers didn't show you."

Thomas interrupted, "John, before we go too much further, I would like to know something. You've said you believe that liberals may someday round up Christians and execute them like Hitler did the Jews. What is their motive? Why are they targeting Christians? Why would they want to do that?"

"It's not very complicated. Actually it's quite simple. As I mentioned earlier today, it's hatred. They hate the one true God and what He represents. God is righteousness, and liberals want to be evil. They want to be able to rape our children and have sex with whomever or whatever, steal what belongs to another, and not feel guilty. That's why one of their biggest arguments is that we Christians shouldn't pawn off our morals on them. They want to be evil and not be held responsible for their acts. As true Christians, we represent the Living God. Liberals hate Christians and Christianity. Jews will be next on their list, but for now Christians are their target of animosity. I told you earlier that liberals are a hate group."

"That's it?"

"Does there need to be more? People have been killing people because of self-serving hatred for centuries. Why would this liberal hate group be any different? Hitler did it."

Thomas didn't have anything else to add or ask, so John continued with the investigation.

"What do you know about homosexuality?"

Thomas shrugged, "Well, homosexuals are naturally at-tracted to members of their same sex. There's not much more to know except maybe that women are called lesbians, and people who are against them are called homophobic."

"Hmm, okay. You said 'naturally attracted.' The gay rights movement is selling what they call the gay gene theory. They are trying to convince society that they are born gay. Unlike the recessive genes that cause baldness, colorblindness, or hemophilia that scientists can pinpoint, scientists have never been able to find a gene that causes homosexuality. You can bet this isn't from their lack of trying.

"How about the mutated gene theory?"

Thomas wore a blank expression on his face, so John continued.

"This theory states that homosexuals result from a mutated gene. Supposedly the exact same piece of information on the DNA code has mutated for all persons who now claim to be homosexual. As you know, the DNA code is the chemical building blocks that contain billions of pieces of information. The mathematical probability of the same mutation occurring at the same time is astronomical—over a billion to one. But let's be liberal with our math, shall we, and say that the chance is one in a hundred million. These are very generous odds. That would account for only seventy homosexuals if the world population is seven billion. That's probably fewer than you'd find in one gay bar in San Francisco. It definitely doesn't explain the hundreds of thousands of homosexuals around the world. Anyone with a brain, who's willing to give it some thought, will rule out that homosexuality is a natural attraction.

"Other indications in the homosexual community itself show even they don't believe it's natural. At Berkeley they have classes that teach men how to be homosexuals. Again the question for anyone who has a brain would be: If it's natural, why do they have to teach it in a class?"

John was not looking for an answer; he just wanted to get Thomas thinking again. He continued, "Two summers ago I got a job at the Lewis and Clark Caverns. I spoke with one of the regular tour guides there, an older gentleman who was also a volunteer AIDS counselor. His son had died of AIDS a couple of years before.

"I had asked him why the AIDS epidemic was growing so rapidly. 'Because homosexuals have so many partners,' he told me. 'They are not interested in monogamous relationships.' I asked, 'Yes, but when they find out they have AIDS, or test HIV-positive, don't they quit having sex and tell their partners so they can get checked?' Carl said, 'They don't quit having sex, and they normally don't tell their partners.' I was appalled. The concept of knowingly endangering another person's life and subjecting them to pain and suffering was beyond me. I couldn't understand how anyone could do such a thing.

"Carl said, 'You have to understand the homosexual mind-set. It's totally different from a normal person's mind-set. While you and I would think of the other person, the homosexual is interested in satisfying only his own desires. That's the only thing that is important to him.' This came from a man whose goal was to comfort those dying of AIDS.

"That same summer I was horseback riding with some friends. On this particular day they had a friend from Denver visiting and riding one of their horses. As we rode I found out that she was a nurse who worked with the state health department. She told me that her job involved going from gay bar to gay bar to make sure her patients took their medications for their various STDs. I kid you not, that really was her job." John responded to a look of doubt that Thomas had given him.

"As she seemed to think I knew something of the homosexual culture, I said to her, 'At least you don't have to track down the lesbians because they're a clean society.' She looked at me like I was an idiot. She asked, 'Why do you think that?' I told her, 'Because they don't have the usual means of transferring the disease.' She enlightened me concerning the homosexual culture. When a lesbian felt wronged by a partner, it was a common practice to have sex with a member of the opposite sex as a way to get even. Since lesbians hang out with male friends from these same gay bars, the diseases spread rapidly.

"Which hurts worse—a punch in the nose or a trust destroyed? The punch in the nose may sting more initially, but the pain soon fades. But a broken heart hurts just as much—and it may hurt for years. That's why at one time adultery was a felony. But this is the culture that our liberal society is selling and demanding we buy into as an alternative lifestyle. Does this lifestyle sound like a civilized behavior that we should promulgate and teach our children, or does it sound dysfunctional?"

"It sounds dysfunctional," Thomas said. "But do all homosexuals practice such vile behavior?"

"Personally I hope not. Usually there are exceptions to the rule. But this 'It's all about me, and it doesn't matter how much pain, suffering, and death I inflict' attitude is the homosexual lifestyle. Homosexuality is a social disorder—not an alternative lifestyle. Psychology classified it as such until enough liberals infiltrated the profession. Through peer pressure and political pressure, homosexuality was taken off the list of mental illnesses. Some true scientists recognize homosexuality for what it is, however, and treat it as a mental illness. Some have successfully cured some ex-homosexuals."

Something John had said puzzled Thomas, so he asked him, "What do you mean by you personally hope not?"

"Do you remember my brother Benjamin?"

"Yeah, I met him at your brother Zeke's funeral."

Zeke had joined the Army a year after graduating from high school. Right after high school he had worked at a lumber mill and had served on the mission field with some members of their church. He was part of a group called Mission Builders International. Zeke was torn between two careers—to be a cop, like his dad, or to join the ministry. He decided to join the Army and become a M.P. In this way he could figure out which was best for him.

Zeke was in the last of his four-year enlistment when the war with Iraq broke out. He had remained stateside when the invasion of Afghanistan took place. He wasn't deployed with the first wave of troops to Iraq, but he went with the second wave. Not long into the war the Iraqi army collapsed, and America took Baghdad. Soon President Bush declared a cease-fire. Many military men in Iraq knew this cease-fire, basically America declaring the war over, came too soon. In the following months while America rebuilt Iraq, insurgents kept shooting at or blowing up our troops. More American troops lost their lives during this cease-fire than in the actual war.

Two weeks after Thanksgiving, Zeke Watchman and his unit patrolled a part of Baghdad called Adhamiya. Their objective was to draw fire by insurgents, so as to locate them and destroy them. Basically the patrol was a decoy. Nobody saw who threw the hand grenade, but it passed through the gunner's port on the top of Zeke's Humvee. Zeke was riding shotgun, carrying an M-16A2, when he heard the grenade land between him and his driver. He quickly picked it up, yelling, "Grenade!" as he tried to throw it out his vehicle door. Zeke was too late. He absorbed most of the blast, leaving his buddies with minor injuries. Zeke had a closed casket ceremony at his funeral.

The gang had been able to attend the funeral as Zeke, Sr. and Ruth had his body brought back to Butte. John's brother Benjamin and his friend Stu had driven from Albuquerque, New Mexico to attend the funeral. Thomas had met both of them at the wake and the dinner that followed.

John said, "Benjamin is gay, and Stu is his partner. Although he used to live that sordid lifestyle, for his sake I hope he's put that all aside. Although I condemn the lifestyle, I love my brother. I even like Stu."

Thomas sat back in his chair with his mouth open. He finally said, "He doesn't look gay. But you, John, I used to think were a little homophobic."

At that John snorted a half laugh and shook his head. He said, "Tom, the homosexual movement advances through two characteristics—ignorance and deceit—and the use of the word homophobic emphasizes the degree of stupidity involved. Liberals say homophobia is a social disease. That might actually be true, not in the way they mean it to be, but in the true meaning of the word. First let me explain why the term homophobic, as it is used today, is a monument to stupidity.

"Back in the sixties and early seventies, when the homosexual movement started, those against the movement called homosexuals 'homos' as a derogatory name. Soon the name calling started. Someone coming to the aid of the homosexual community, showing their ignorance, added *phobia* to the derogative *homo*. The press picked up on the word and coined the term *homophobic*. A poor neologism at best.

"Let's break down the word and see why I find the term humorous as it's used. The prefix is derived from the Greek word *homos* meaning same. Many people mistakenly believe that the Latin translation of *homo*, meaning man, was used. People mistakenly believe that homosexual refers to a sexual attraction to men. If you give it half a thought, even straight women would then be classified as homosexuals. That's definitely a no-brainer. Because the prefix is rooted in the Greek translation, the true meaning is a sexual attraction to the same sex.

"Now let's look at the other half of the word. A phobia is a persistent, illogical, or abnormal fear. Those of the pro-homosexual movement who use the term, do so incorrectly. They claim that anyone who disagrees or opposes homosexuality is phobic. If you study, and ask questions about the lifestyle of homosexuals, you can only conclude that homosexuality is immoral and socially unacceptable. That is, for a civilized society. This conclusion is not based on fear, anger, or hate. It is based on moral decency. As the term homophobic is used today, it is merely name calling, such as dummy, jerk, or knucklehead, which in itself is a form of hatred.

"When you break down the word homophobic, it actually means the same fear, or a fear common to all. Give it some thought. What fear is prevalent in our society as a whole?" Thomas just shrugged. John answered, "I think the only unreasonable fear festering in our society is the fear of being held responsible for our own actions. This fear is universal and affects every niche of our society."

Thomas wore a doubtful expression.

"You think I'm wrong? When you're speeding and a cop has you on his radar, do you believe you should get a ticket? How many excuses can you think of for not obeying simple traffic laws? The degree of fear of responsibility just escalates from there. It's the true meaning of homophobia, the same or common fear that has allowed the homosexual movement to advance the way it has. If men don't have to

118

be ashamed of sexual intercourse with another man, how much easier it is for us to justify the sinful acts we commit. Homophobia—the best thing to ever happen for the advancement of the homosexual movement."

"John, you have a way of bringing a new perspective on things. I never would have thought of it like that before."

"Of course not. The public schools and media have programmed you to think that everyone who condemns homosexuality is a hate-filled, religious Christian bigot. I said earlier that one of the liberal's main weapons is deceit. The truth of the matter is we're educated, and they despise that. Have you ever noticed how the liberals attribute their characteristics to anyone they hate? They use to call this a Freudian slip. Freud said people see others as they see themselves. Modern psychologists reject this theory because Freud predominantly studied the criminally insane. I feel it is appropriate where liberals are concerned, however.

"Now let's look at the claims of the liberal party that gays were historically persecuted by 'homophobic heterosexual Nazis,' who gave them their pink triangle symbol. This is actually a lie. What's the truth? Homosexual Nazis persecuted homosexuals."

"But why would they do that? It does not make sense."

"It does when you've educated yourself to the true nature of homosexuality. Remember I mentioned there were different types of homosexuals?"

"Yeah."

"Some are called Femmes and some are called Butch. The Germans of Hitler's Third Reich used the same terms. *The Pink Swastika*, a book written by two historians named Scott Lively and Kevin Abrams, describes the Nazi party in detail. This article that I'm using was written by Scott Lively.

The two factions hate each other. My brother Benjamin confirmed this for me.

"Let's look at history again to get the full understanding of what took place in Nazi Germany—the real birthplace of the modern gay rights movement." John paraphrased as he read, "'The founder was a homosexual German lawyer by the name of Karl Heinrich Ulrichs. Ulrichs had been molested at the age of fourteen by his male riding instructor. Instead of attributing his adult homosexuality to the molestation, Ulrich devised in the 1860s the "third sex" theory of homosexuality. Ulrich said male homosexuals are actually female souls trapped within male bodies. The reverse was supposed to be true for lesbians. Ulrich argued that because it was an innate condition, homosexuality should be decriminalized.' Sound familiar?

"'By 1895, the German gay rights had gained strength. Frederich Engels, a socialist, wrote in a letter to Karl Marx regarding Ulrich's efforts. The pederasts started counting their numbers and discovered they are a powerful group in our state. The only thing missing is an organization, but it seems to exist already, but it is hidden.'

"By Engel's letter, Tom, you can see that a secret society had already started. After Ulrich's death in 1895, the movement split into two different and opposing groups. The first group was organized by Magnus Hirschfeld, who formed the Scientific Humanitarian Committee in 1897 and later opened the Institute for Sex Research in Berlin. Hirschfeld's group embraced Ulrich's theory of a feminine identity. His followers believed they were women trapped in men's bodies. These effeminate homosexuals are the Femmes.

"It's the second group that caused the problems. This group was organized by Adolf Brand, Benedict Friedlander, and Wilhelm Janzen who, in 1902, formed the *Gemeinschaft der Eigenen* or the Community of the Special. This group asserted that male homosexuality was the foundation of all nation-states and male homosexuals represented the elite of human society. The Community of the Special, or the CS, was ultra-masculine, male-supremacist, and pederasts devoted to having sex with boys.

"Brand wrote in his magazine, The *Der Eigene*, or *The Special*, that they wanted men who thirsted for a revival of Greek times and Hellenic standards of beauty after centuries of Christian barbarism. Does that sound familiar, Tom? The gay rights movement of the Nazis called Christians barbarian. Today's version calls us bigots and homophobic."

Thomas simply nodded and waited to listen to the rest of this. He found this interesting. John continued, "These are the Butch homosexuals. Because of their super male egos, they despised the Femmes. This Butch faction also became the driving force of the Nazi party, and they recruited their members from the German version of the boy scouts. In the 1890s, an informal hiking and camping group called the *Wandervogel* became an official organization at the turn of the century. The co-founder of the Community of the Special, Wilhelm Janzen, took control of the *Wandervogel* early in its growth. The boys were indoctrinated with Greek paganism and taught to reject the Christian values of their parents. Sounds like many public schools today, doesn't it? The primary function of the *Wandervogel*, through this indoctrination and by molestation, was to teach these boys to be homosexuals.

"Later, during World War I, a homosexual army officer, Gerhard Rossbach, transformed the *Wandervogel* into the German Storm Troopers, also known as the Brown Shirts. The term 'der Fuehrer,' meaning the leader, and the Seig Heil salute originated in the *Wandervogel*. Ernst Roehm, another homosexual and member of the Community of the Special who was recruited by Rossbach, became the first leader of the Nazi party and commander of the Storm Troopers. Lively writes to become a high-ranking officer in the Storm Troopers, you had to be a homosexual. Roehm publicly flaunted his homosexuality and projected a social order in which homosexuality would be regarded as a human behavior pattern of high repute.

"Roehm believed the Nazis needed a proud and arrogant lot who could brawl, carouse, smash windows, kill, and slaughter without remorse. Straights, in his eyes, were not as adept in such behavior as practicing homosexuals. 'The primary purpose of Roehm's Storm Troopers was beating up anyone who opposed the Nazis, and Hitler believed this was a job best undertaken by homosexuals.' Get this—Roehm was a prominent member of the Society for Human Rights, an offshoot of the Community of the Special.

"Tom, earlier you asked me about conspiracies. Listen to what is written here. 'The favorite meeting place of the SA...' SA was the acronym for *Sturmabteilung* or in English, Storm Troopers," John explained. He quickly skimmed through much of the material, going over only the highlights of the article, and had left out most of the acronyms. For some reason John despised acronyms.

John started over, "'The favorite meeting place of the SA was a "gay" bar in Munich called The Bratwurstglockl where Roehm kept a reserved table. This was the same tavern where some of the earliest formative meetings of the Nazi party had been held. At the Bratwurstglockl, Roehm and associates—Edmund Heines, Karl Ernst, Ernst's partner, Captain Rohrbein, Captain Petersdor, Count Ernst Helldorf, and the rest—would meet to plan and strategize. These were the men who orchestrated the Nazi campaign of intimidation and terror. All of them were homosexual. Heinrick Himmler complained once, "Does it not constitute a danger to the Nazi movement if it can be said that

122

Nazi leaders are chosen for sexual reasons?" Himmler wasn't against homosexuality; he was against the fact that non-qualified people were given high rank based on their homosexual relations with Roehm and others. An example would be Karl Ernst. He had been a hotel doorman and a waiter prior to becoming a general in the Storm Troopers and described as a common thug. By 1933, the Storm Troopers had grown larger than the German army with Roehm in charge of over 2,500,000 troops. One historian, H. R. Knickerbocker, wrote that Roehm had surrounded himself with a staff of perverts. The Vikingkorps, officers' corps, was almost exclusively homosexual.'"

"I was always taught that Hitler denounced homosexuality," Thomas interrupted.

"Publicly he did. He even had Roehm executed, claiming it was because of his homosexuality. It was all a lie! But we're getting ahead of ourselves, and that will all be explained a little later.

"I guess now is as good a time as any to see how Hitler fits into all this. A lot of circumstantial evidence indicates that Hitler himself practiced homosexuality, but not exclusively. He is known to have had sexual relationships with at least four women. All four women tried to commit suicide after becoming his lover, and two of them succeeded.

"Hitler was a coprophile, meaning he was aroused by human excrement. Langer, a psychiatrist hired by the Allies to study Hitler, suggested that Hitler's sexual escapades with women included expressions of his coprophilic perversion as well as other extremely degrading forms of masochism. One thing is absolutely certain. Hitler preferred the company of homosexuals and surrounded himself with staff members who were homosexuals or bisexual.

"Hitler started out as a protégé of Roehm. Roehm had been highly placed in the underground nationalist

movement that plotted to overthrow the Weiman government and worked to subvert it through assassination and
terrorism. Roehm met Hitler at a meeting of a socialist
terrorist group called the Iron Fist and saw in Hitler the
demagogue he required to mobilize mass support for his
secret army. Roehm, who had joined the German Worker's
Party before Hitler, worked with him to take over the fledg-
ling organization. With Roehm's backing Hitler became the
first president of the party in 1921, and changed its name
to the National Socialist German Worker's Party. Soon after,
Rossbach's Storm Troopers became its military arm.

"Hitler's rise to power could not have happened without
the gay rights movement. Hitler needed Roehm and the
contributions from Roehm's wealthy homosexual support-
ers. Hitler may have been a bisexual, but he was definitely a
politician. Public outcry about the obscene behavior of the
Storm Troopers and the Nazi party exerted some pressure.
Political pressure outside the Nazi party, namely from Mus-
solini, also forced Hitler's hand to denounce homosexual
practices. So in 1933, Hitler publicly banned pornography,
homosexual bars and bath houses, and groups that promoted gay rights. He used a German law that was in effect
long before the Nazi regime. Paragraph 175 of the Reich
Criminal Code prohibited sodomy. Hitler used this law to
his advantage to imprison political enemies.

"Hitler openly opposed homosexuality for other reasons. On May 6, 1933, Roehm's Storm Troopers attacked
the Magnus Hirschfelder Sex Research Institute, destroyed
it, and stole numerous documents. What was the reason
for the raid? Ludwig L. Lenz, the assistant director of the
Sex Research Institute who was in charge on the day it was
raided, said, 'Our Institute was used by all classes of the
population and members of every political party.... . We thus
had a great many Nazis under treatment at the Institute.

Why was it then, since we were completely non-party, that our purely scientific Institute was the first victim which fell to the new regime? The answer to this is simple.... We knew too much. It would be against medical principles to provide a list of the Nazi leaders and their perversions but, not ten percent of the men who, in 1933, took the fate of Germany into their hands were sexually normal.... Many of these personages were known to us directly through consultations; we heard about others from their comrades in the party... and of others we saw the tragic results.... Our knowledge of such intimate secrets regarding members of the Nazi party and other documentary material, we possessed about forty thousand confessions and biographical letters, was the cause of the complete and utter destruction of the Institute of Sexology.'

"Tom, you know the 'book burning' that the Nazis are noted for? The documents from this institute were burned. Another common phenomenon within the homosexual community was blackmailing. Estranged partners and male prostitutes blackmailed former lovers and threatened them with public exposure. This was actually quite common. So when Hitler started his persecution against the homosexual community, it wasn't because of their sexual preference; it was because they posed a threat to him and the Nazi party.

"The Butch homosexuals of the Nazi party also targeted the Femme homosexuals for a show of enforcement of Hitler's ban. But this was very selective. Many were spared because of their talents in the fine arts. One example of this was actor Gustaf Grundgens. Goering appointed him director of the State Theater.

"On June 28, 1934, Hitler had some of his closest aides orchestrate the assassination of hundreds of his political enemies. This is known as the Night of the Long Knives or the Roehm Purge. Hitler claimed it was a 'moral cleansing' of the Nazi ranks. He lied. It was because of Roehm's sway over the Storm Troopers, and the *Wehrmacht*, the German Army High Command, feared that he might seize control of the army. Roehm had become a menace to Hitler. So he had him and about a thousand other political enemies killed. The majority of the men who did the killing were homosexuals themselves: Wagner, Esser, Maurice, Weber, and Buch.

"You see, Tom, of the five to fifteen thousand homosexuals who were imprisoned in the German concentration camps—and only a small amount of those died there—most were there for political reasons. Many weren't even homosexuals. They were just accused of that so they could be put in prison without too many questions. Those who persecuted them were homosexuals; those who killed them were homosexuals; even the camp commandant, Rudolf Hoess, was a homosexual. Today's liberals claim historical persecution of homosexuals. That's hogwash. Persecution didn't occur at the hands of heterosexual Christian bigots. Homosexuals with perverted minds persecuted their own kind."

"This all sounds so diabolical," Thomas said.

"It was diabolical! If you think today's liberals aren't just as or even more diabolical, you're fooling yourself. I want to read you two more paragraphs from this article. 'Much had been made of the reported silence, and in some cases complicity, of the supposed Christian churches during the Third Reich. But few have noted the long period of "Biblical deconstruction" that preceded the rise of Nazism, and fewer still have chronicled the diabolical perversion of German religious culture by the Nazis themselves. While the neo-pagans were busy attacking from without, liberal theologians undermined biblical authority from within the

Christian church. The school of so-called "higher criticism," which began in Germany in the late 1800s, portrayed the miracles of God as myths; by implication making true believers (Jews and Christians alike) into fools. Since the Bible was no longer accepted as God's divine and inerrant guide, it could be ignored or reinterpreted. By the time the Nazis came to power "Bible-believing" Christians (the Confessing Church) were a small minority. As Grunberger asserts, Nazism itself was a "pseudo-religion" that competed, in a sense, with Christianity and Judaism.'

"The modern version of Nazism today, Tom, is humanism. The last paragraph I want to read is this: 'The probable reason for Hitler's attack on Christianity was his perception that it alone had the moral authority to stop the Nazi movement. But Christians stumbled before the flood of evil. As Poliakov notes, "When moral barriers collapsed under the impact of Nazi preaching... The same anti-Semitic movement that led to the slaughter of the Jews gave scope and license to an obscene revolt against God and the moral law. An open and implacable war was declared on the Christian tradition... [which unleashed] a frenzied and un-avowed hatred of Christ and the Ten Commandments."'

"Tell me, Tom, doesn't this sound exactly like America today? The way the Nazis tore down the Christian faith back then is exactly how the liberals are doing it here and now. Sounds like history repeating itself, doesn't it? And if liberals are willing to repeat that part of history, why wouldn't they be willing to repeat the holocaust as well?"

While John had been reading how the Christian faith had been undermined, Thomas had thought to himself that it was sounding like modern America. John's questions just honed the perception. This was all so new to him. Thomas just shook his head and answered in a low tone, "I don't know."

John decided to see how much of this Thomas was getting. He said, "It's time for a pop quiz, Tom. Question one: The Sex Research Institute was studying sexual behavior for fourteen years before Hitler shut them down. After fourteen years of intense research, what did the assistant director call their patient's sexual habits?" John looked to Thomas and raised an eyebrow to indicate he was waiting for an answer.

Thomas thought for a few seconds, but his mind drew a blank. So he smiled and jokingly asked, "Is this an open book quiz?"

To Thomas's surprise John opened the article to the right page and said, "The answer is in the last paragraph in parentheses."

Thomas took the article and read silently to himself.

"Oh, he called them perversions."

"Right! Question two: What was said about the men who took the fate of Germany into their own hands?"

Thomas had just read the answer. He said, "That not ten percent were sexually normal."

"Right again. Next question. What can you deduce by the comments of Ludwig Lenz, the assistant director of the Sex Research Institute who most likely was a homosexual himself?"

Thomas thought about this for a moment and what John had said earlier. It made a little more sense now. Thomas answered, "That homosexuality is a social disorder and not a lifestyle."

"Not a lifestyle acceptable for any civilized society at least. There is an interesting quote by Rudolf Hoess, the Butch homosexual who ran Auschwitz. He defined the effeminate homosexuals, or Femmes, as genuine homosexuals by their soft and girlish affections and fastidiousness, their sickly sweet manner of speech, and their altogether too affectionate deportment toward their fellows. Note how a Butch homosexual calls a Femme homosexual genuine.

"Believe it or not, there are actually some good psychologists who are still real scientists. There is the National Association for Research and Therapy of Homosexuality, in California of all places, founded by Joseph J. Nicolosi. These scientists still classify homosexuality as a mental illness. They have treated several homosexuals and cured them. This is news the liberal community does not want to get out, so they deny it emphatically. These scientists have discovered that genuine homosexuals are a product of bad parenting. The mental condition is ingrained at a very early age, as young as three and four, I believe. Overall, parents of genuine homosexuals consist of an overbearing mother combined with a father who is either absent, neglectful, or degrading. A common trait of all genuine homosexuals is that they hated their fathers growing up. This shows that homosexuality is not hereditary, or at least not passed on through the gene pool, but is a learned trait or mental condition."

"I'm kind of curious. Would your brother Benjamin be considered a Femme or a Butch homosexual?"

John could see the question was earnest and said, "My parents had some hard times when Benjamin was born. My father, an unbeliever then, had pretty much abandoned Mom and Benjamin. My mom was forced to act like both Mom and Dad. Dad didn't get saved until a few years after Benjamin was born. I guess it was about the time little Zeke was born. My mom said she was pretty much ready to leave him just before he came back to his senses.

"Benjamin had the right environment as a child to produce homosexual traits, but I also know that he was sexually molested when he was seventeen. He told me he initiated it, but I don't know. Benjamin is easily led, then claims it was his idea. Anyway, he could be a little of both, I guess. One thing was for sure, Dad and Benjamin were never close while we were growing up. I think it's time to get back to the quiz though. What question are we on?"

"Three or four, I think. I hope this isn't twenty questions."

"Don't worry, just two more to keep your brain working. I don't want you to fall asleep on me. Or I'll leave you here so you'll miss the movie tonight."

"I bet you would. You're such a kind friend," Thomas retorted.

"Question four," John smiled. "You can reference the last page with the lower corner bent. What are modern liberals in America saying about the miracles of God that is identical to what the liberals of Germany before the Nazi holocaust were saying about them?"

Thomas didn't have to read too much. The answer was at the top of the page. "They called them myths, by implication making true believers to appear as fools."

John emphasized his earlier statement and said, "Very good! You're batting a thousand so far. Do you notice their tactics back then are the same as they are now, or vice versa? They infiltrate the ranks of their enemies and subvert them from within. You know what the miracle is? Jesus predicted they would two thousand years ago."

Thomas nodded.

"Last question. You'll find the answer on the same page, fourth paragraph. What item have modern liberal judges banned from schools and courthouses, and what do you think is the driving force behind their motivation to do so?"

The first part of this question was easy to answer. The second half caused Thomas to hesitate before answering. He read the paragraph a couple of times to himself and started to form an answer. Hitler's attack on Christianity... he perceived it alone had the moral authority to stop the Nazi movement. When moral barriers collapse... the same anti-semitic movement that led to the slaughter of the Jews gave scope and license to revolt against God and moral law... implacable war declared on Christian tradition... unleashing frenzied and unavowed hatred of Christ and the Ten Commandments. That was it. Thomas had thought the answer to the second part of the question was going to be hard, but it wasn't. It was easy.

"The item the judges have banned is the Ten Commandments. The driving force is hatred. The proof is the passion they display when ruling a religious placard or display as unconstitutional."

"Wow! You passed that quiz with flying colors. Here's some more proof that liberal judges are ruling based on their hatred of God and Christ. Haven't judges banned prayer in public schools?"

"Yes, they have."

"And what was their excuse for this ban?"

"They say it's because of the separation of church and state."

"That is a lie! And it's as transparent a lie as the one Hitler gave when he called the Roehm purging a moral cleansing. With both, you just need to look at the history of how they were implemented. Hitler and his group selected whom they declared homosexual and imprisoned. Modern liberal judges select which religion they persecute. Basically, judges won't allow the mention of God or Christ in schools. But there has been no problem with a kid mentioning Buddha, Gaia, Satan, or allowing teachers to practice and teach new age humanism, which if my memory serves me right was classified as a religion, or Hindu practices such as meditation and yoga. Pretty much all separation of church and state is directed at Christians and Christianity. The liberal courts say they are upholding the Constitution by prohibiting Christians from praying in school. Have you ever read the First Amendment?"

Thomas may have read it in school one time, but he could not remember it. He shook his head no. John reached in his backpack and pulled out his copy of the Constitution. He thumbed through it and, finding what he was looking for, read, "'Article One: Congress shall make no law respecting an establishment of religion, or prohibiting the free exercise thereof…' Did you happen to catch the last six words I just said—'or prohibiting the free exercise thereof? It means just what it says."

"Well, it sounds to me like they can't make any laws prohibiting prayer in schools."

"That's exactly what it means," John said.

Thomas looked a little confused. If the Constitution prohibited it, how could the courts enact such laws?

"John, how can such laws be made and kept?"

"Well, you have a Christian-hating activist whine to the courts. Christian-hating liberal judges rule in favor of the whiner. Christian-hating liberal educators enforce the 'court law,' and a Christian-hating liberal media publicly bashes anyone who attempts to right a wrong."

Although true, that wasn't the answer Thomas was looking for. He wasn't looking for an over-simplified version of what was going on. He wanted to know how an entity of the government could violate the very Constitution it was supposed to protect.

John knew it. He knew what Thomas was looking for. He wanted to emphasize that multiple groups were working together to reach a common goal. John said, "What you really want are the arguments the courts used to subvert the system, right?"

"That's right, wise guy," Thomas said in feigned disgust.

"It's not all that hard," John said. "I believe I told you once that the greatest allies of the liberal movement are ignorance and deceit, didn't I?"

"I think you were talking about the gay rights movement at the time."

"Same thing. Don't let semantics confuse you. When you look at the big picture, all the different liberal groups, regardless of what they advocate or call themselves, are fighting for the same goal—the annihilation of God and His people. This is how liberal judges get away with it. Do you ever recall hearing those last six words before: 'or prohibiting the free exercise thereof?'"

"No, I don't think I have."

"Not by the media or a teacher or a quote in the papers by a judge?"

Thomas sat back and crossed his arms. "No, I don't recall ever hearing that part of the Constitution before."

"The vast majority of the people in America haven't. Although that same majority will swear they know their constitutional rights, few truly do. Liberal judges know this, so they use our ignorance against us. They also use deceit. Let's look at the first part of Amendment One. 'Congress shall make no law respecting an establishment of religion.' Do you see anywhere in there the words 'separation of church and state'?"

"No."

"Do you know the definition of establishment as it is used here?"

"Yes, of course. It means to institute by law."

"Very good. Have you ever seen the word separation in the definition of the word establishment?"

"No," Thomas said again. He recalled that John had broached this subject earlier and then let it die. He was eager to hear John's explanation.

"That's because it's not there. The first part of this amendment doesn't advocate a separation of church and state. It means just what it says. The federal government and—thanks to the Fourteenth Amendment—state governments can't establish one religion to be practiced against the will of the people. The government can't make Catholicism or Buddhism or Hinduism the national religion. They can't make everyone follow the Baptist religion. This clause was a reaction against the English tradition of the king declaring a Church of England or national church. The term 'separation of church and state' came from a law drafted by Thomas Jefferson. It was designed to prevent the government from interfering with church business, not the other way around as it is now being used. But how many people in America do you think know about this law?"

"Not too many. I know I never heard about it."

"You're right. So the liberal courts twist the meaning of this law, mix it with the First Amendment, taint some evidence—the letter by Thomas Jefferson to the Danbury Baptist Church—and come up with a ruling that suits their purpose. By the way, just so you don't think this is just a matter of my opinion, you should know that the Supreme Court addressed this issue in 1878 in *George Reynolds v. US*. At that time, when the bench wasn't infected with Christian-hating liberal judges, they ruled that there was not a separation of church and state."

Thomas looked shocked.

"I don't have that case with me, but you can look it up for yourself. It's *George Reynolds v. US, 1878*. But do you see how history has a way of repeating itself? Everything the liberals and Nazis of Germany did during and before World

War II is being done by today's liberals. They exhibit the same tactics, the same hatred. How could it turn out any other way but by them rounding up God-fearing people and executing them just like Hitler and his group exterminated the Jews? I haven't even scratched the surface of all the evidence to prove our case that liberals will commit genocide again."

CHAPTER 7

STILL MORE EVIDENCE

Let's take a look at evolution, shall we? There is no such thing as a creation-believing liberal, is there?" asked John.

"No, there's not. But you have to admit Darwin's theory of evolution is hard to dispute."

"Is it?" John asked mockingly. "Au contraire, my friend, au contraire. If you truly look at all the scientific evidence and not the lies that the liberals spread, you'll find it takes more faith to believe in Darwinism, more faith by far, than it does to believe in Christ."

"I saw a documentary about evolution on television just a couple of years ago, and it was filled with some undisputable facts about evolution and Darwin's theory."

"Undisputable? Thomas, I keep telling you that the liberal cause advances through deceit and ignorance. I've also told you that the media is a major player in the liberal's cause just as it was for Hitler. I saw that same show, *Evolution*, the miniseries. And you want to know something? They lied!"

John reached into his backpack and pulled out a hardback book with a predominately orange and yellow cover. He held it up and said, "Tom, a lot of books on the market today are written by established, prominent scientists. They span a wide range of the scientific disciplines such as astronomy, cosmology, embryology, biochemistry, and the like. Do you know the common theme of all these books?" John waited for Thomas to reply. Thomas just shook his head no, so John continued, "They all come to the same conclusion that this world, this universe and everything it contains, is a product of intelligent design. Or more simply, it was created. Some of these scientists claim that the evidence gathered so far not only points to the world and universe being designed, but they are designed for life on this planet alone. All the evidence that has been gathered within the past fifty years points to and promotes the theory of creation. We're talking about empirical science. This is science that can be tested.

"On the other hand, Darwinists or evolutionists or humanists or liberals, whatever you want to call them, are grasping at straws. They are desperate to find one real piece of evidence that could validate evolution. But the more they dig, the more the evidence leads away from evolution. It's so bad for them, Tom, that a large market exists for fabricated fossils. I believe China and Mexico are producing these fakes, but evolutionists are so desperate for proof that they are paying big bucks for them. It's getting so bad that I see a time when no archeological find will even be considered—unless a video shows the start of a dig to the excavation of the find, and only if the video is authenticated by a group of unbiased scientists throughout its making.

"This book by Lee Strobel, *A Case for the Creator*, is by a journalist who interviews a number of scientists, scientists who themselves have written books promoting intelligent design and who explain some of the Darwin myths and expound on all the facts that prove creation."

"I read *A Case for Christ*," Thomas interrupted. "It was a very compelling book. He did pretty much the same thing in that book. I mean with the interview style of writing."

"Good, so you're familiar with his style. That will make this easier. I want to read some of the passages to show you where or how some of the Darwin myths are still being promoted by the mainstream media and education institutes. Then I want to read about some of the evidence showing that creation is the best answer."

Thomas had this gut-wrenching feeling that all he had learned in school was about to be proven a bunch of worthless hogwash. He wondered why he even attended the past six years of public school.

John decided to do all the reading for the sake of time. He wanted to go to the grocery store before the group met for dinner, and he still had a lot of material to cover. John opened the book to a pre-marked page and cleared his throat.

"We need to ask ourselves several questions. One: Which way does empirical science lean, toward creation or evolution? Two: If the evidence shows that evolution is a false theory and points strongly toward creation, why isn't it being taught in our schools and revealed by the media? Three: Why are liberals so frantic about denying the evidence and lying about what they have? Lee Strobel's book starts out with what he calls the four images of evolution. Teachers use these same four subjects today to show young impressionable minds how we and everything else on this planet evolved.

"The first image Strobel covers is the 1953 Stanley Miller Experiment. Miller reproduced what he believed was primitive earth's atmosphere and, by utilizing electric sparks that simulated lightning, also produced a red goo containing amino acids, which are the building blocks of life. The second image Strobel talks about is Darwin's Tree of Life. This was Darwin's illustration of how life started from one form and over a period of time branched into the vast variety of life we know today. This is the process of natural selection acting as a catalyst for all life forms; the 'man from monkey' thing. The third image Strobel writes about is Ernst Haeckel's drawings of embryos. This German biologist said he sketched drawings of embryos of a fish, salamander, tortoise, chick, hog, calf, rabbit, and human, and put them side by side to show the world how alike they were, insinuating that we all shared a common ancestry. The fourth image Strobel writes about is the missing link, archaeopteryx. This creature had wings, feathers, and a wishbone but also had a lizard-like tail and claws on its wings."

Thomas nodded to show he knew what John was talking about. He was familiar with all these images. He had first learned about them in grade school, and they were reiterated all the way though high school. On more than one occasion, it had made Thomas wonder if the beliefs he had learned in church had been true. He questioned his mother, a devout Catholic, about it once. She told him that God used evolution as a way to create life, and the Bible just told people what they could understand back in the old days. It had helped him keep his belief in God but gave him doubts about how trustworthy the Bible was.

"Before we look more closely at these four images," John continued, "I want to establish some traits of science that Strobel also established early in this book." John opened the book to its beginning and turned a few pages. He pointed to a paragraph and read at the same time to emphasize his point. "'Science, said two-time Nobel Prize winner, Linus

Pauling, is the search for the truth.' Remember what we discussed about absolute truth earlier today?"

"Yeah," Thomas nodded.

"If there were no absolute truth, science would be useless." John turned his attention to the opposite page and read, "'Scientists themselves will tell you that this is entirely appropriate. "All scientific knowledge," said no less an authority than the National Academy of Sciences, "is, in principle, subject to change as new evidence becomes available."' Remember, Tom, absolute truth is based on the accumulation of facts and evidence. With a small amount of evidence one might deduce a logical conclusion, but as more evidence is found, an entirely different conclusion can be derived. The key is the accumulated facts."

Although Thomas nodded his understanding, his blank expression led John to elaborate with an example.

"This would be like a cop coming across a man stooped over the body of a person who had been murdered. With only that evidence the cop naturally suspects the man. It's a logical conclusion with what little information the officer has. When the coroner's report shows the body had been dead for two days, and the man had been in a different state at the time of the murder, what's the logical conclusion? Someone else murdered the person, and the man happened to find the body just before the cop showed up."

"So the cop arrested the man from his opinion, not from the truth. It kind of shows you how dangerous it is to jump to conclusions."

"Yes, it is. A hundred years ago, because of all of the hypotheses and theories that were prevalent, scientists concluded that science had taken God out of the picture. But with all the new evidence that has been discovered over the past forty to fifty years, true scientists have had to paint Him back into the picture in a way that would make Michelangelo envious."

"John, if new facts can change what is believed to be true, wouldn't that indicate that there is no absolute truth?"

"Not at all," John answered. "A hypothesis is not the same as the truth. With a hypothesis you make assumptions based on limited facts, which you hope will lead you to additional facts, which will lead to the truth. Not all assumptions are correct, and a new hypothesis may be needed to come to a logical conclusion. This is where empirical science comes into play. If a scientist can reproduce a desired effect, his hypothesis is then considered fact. Also the truth can be expanded upon." John rapped his knuckles against the table and said, "I can say in truth that this table is made from a hard piece of material. My knocking on it shows the absolute truth of that statement. By examining the table, with my knowledge of certain material, I determine that the table is wooden. The absolute truth is that the table is made of a hard, wooden material. If a carpenter or botanist tells us what type of wood it is, then we can say the absolute truth is that the table is made of hard oak wood."

"I get it. As long as the statement you make is factual and can't be disputed, it is absolute truth even though you may not have come to the ultimate conclusion."

"That's right," John said. "Let's get back to Strobel's book." John thumbed through the pages and stopped at a place with large, bold letters that Thomas could easily read, even sideways! Interview number one: Jonathan Wells, PhD, PhD. John paused there only a second as if to gain a reference point. John turned a couple more pages then began, "The first scientist whom Strobel interviewed was Jonathan Wells, who has a doctorate in molecular and cell biology with a primary focus on vertebrate embryology and evolution. He also has degrees in geology and physics.

Wells calls Strobel's images 'icons,' which I think is more accurate. Wells said the icons for evolution are either false or misleading."

Thomas put his hand to his chin and leaned closer, his attention becoming even keener. Thomas knew that what he was about to hear would be more of a revelation than he ever expected.

"First, Wells debunked the Miller Experiment. Let me read this. 'Well, nobody knows for sure what the early atmosphere was like, but the consensus is that the atmosphere was not at all like the one Miller used,' he began. 'Miller chose a hydrogen-rich mixture of methane, ammonia, and water vapor which was consistent with what many scientists thought back then. But scientists don't believe that anymore. As a geophysicist with the Carnegie Institution said in the 1960s, "What is the evidence for a primitive methane-ammonia atmosphere on earth? The answer is that there is no evidence for it, but much against it." By the mid 1970s, Belgium biochemist, Marcel Florkin, was declaring that the concept behind Miller's theory of the early atmosphere "has been abandoned.""'"

John skipped some of the material for the sake of time.

"'The best hypothesis now is that there was very little hydrogen in the atmosphere because it would have escaped into space. Instead, the atmosphere probably consisted of carbon dioxide, nitrogen, and water vapor,' Wells said. 'So my gripe is that textbooks still present the Miller experiment as though it reflected the earth's early environment when most geochemists, since the 1960s, would say it was totally unlike Miller's.'"

John looked to Thomas and said, "I have a question I want you to ponder. Do you think it's coincidence that the liberal education system still supplies schools with textbooks with faulty information? As we go through this book you'll see this isn't the only piece of faulty information our liberal education system tries to pass off as factual.

"Wells brings up another interesting fact liberal educators and the media refuse to disclose. Even if amino acids were present, there is no known way to make those amino acids come to life. It's just impossible. Strobel asked the question, 'From amino acids how far is that from life?' I'll read Wells' response: "'Oh," he said as he pounced on the question, "Very far. Incredibly far. That would be the first step in an extremely complicated process. You would have to get the right number of the right kinds of amino acids to link up to create a protein molecule and that would still be a long way from a living cell. Then you'd need dozens of protein molecules, again in the right sequence, to create a living cell. The odds against this are astonishing. The gap between non-living chemicals and even the most primitive living organism is absolutely tremendous! Frankly, the idea that we're on the verge of explaining the origin of life naturalistically is just silly to me.'"

"Strobel has a quote from another origin of life expert, Walter Bradley, that I want to read to you." John turned the page and read, "'If there isn't a natural explanation and there doesn't seem to be the potential of finding one, then I believe it's appropriate to look at a supernatural explanation,' said Bradley. 'I think that's the most reasonable inference based on the evidence.' That's something you won't find printed in a public school textbook."

"No, you won't," Thomas agreed.

"Now," John continued, "let's see what Dr. Wells has to say about the second icon, Darwin's Tree of Life. Strobel asked Wells if Darwin's evolutionary tree held up in light of a century of fossil discoveries. Here is Well's response. "'Absolutely not," came his quick reply. "As an illustration of the fossil record, the Tree of Life is a dismal failure. But it is a good representation of Darwin's theory."'"

"Does he mean Darwin's theory is a dismal failure?" Thomas interrupted.

"Uh, well, no..." John started until he noticed the grin on Thomas's face. John grinned too and conceded, "Maybe, inadvertently. He explains that the biggest problem for the evolutionist is the Cambrian Era. At that time, there suddenly appear arthropods, modern representatives such as insects, crabs, and lobsters. There were modern starfish and sea urchins. There were even chordates, which included modern vertebrates. They all appeared too quickly for Darwin's evolution to have taken place. Wells said the Cambrian explosion has uprooted Darwin's tree. Wells stated that there is no real scientific explanation for it."

Thomas shook his head.

"Mind boggling, isn't it?" John asked.

"Yeah, it truly is. I've always accepted evolution as scientific fact. I've never heard anything to the contrary, except from preachers. I always figured they were doing the religion thing and didn't give them much heed," Thomas said.

"If that was a revelation, you're really going to love the explanation that refutes the third icon, Ernst Haeckel's embryo drawing."

What could be more of an eye-opener? Thomas thought. He asked, "What does Wells say about Haeckel's embryos?"

"Just that they are frauds," John smiled. "And the fact that it was known that they were frauds since the late 1860s when his colleagues accused him of it."

"Hold on," Thomas interrupted. "I was taught about those drawings in my sophomore or junior year in high school. My teacher taught us that the human embryo went through several stages of evolution before it took on human form, and she used these pictures to prove it. Now you're telling me that they have known since the 1860s that they're fakes? If they have known these things are fakes, why on earth are they still teaching lies?"

"You want to hear something funny? Strobel had the same reaction when Wells told him, and Wells stated he had the same reaction when he found out they were frauds. Let's look at your why question in a few minutes. First let's look at the three things that Wells said was wrong with Haeckel's drawings to leave no doubt in your mind that they were scientific frauds. Remember embryology is Wells' specialty.

"First let me read this excerpt: 'There are three problems with these drawings,' he said, 'The first is that the similarities in the early stages were faked...' Apparently in some cases Haeckel used the same woodcut to print embryos from different classes because he was so confident of his theory that he figured he didn't have to draw them separately. In other cases he doctored the drawings to make them look more similar than they really are. At any rate, his drawings misrepresent the embryos. Now let me read Wells' second problem. 'The minor problem is that Haeckel cherry-picked his examples,' Wells explained. 'He only shows a few of the seven vertebrate classes. For example, his most famous rendition had eight columns. Four are mammals, but they're all placental mammals. There are two other kinds of mammals that he didn't show which are different. The remaining four classes he showed—reptiles, birds, amphibians, and fish—happen to be more similar than the ones he omitted. He used a salamander to represent amphibians instead of a frog, which looks very different. So he stacked the deck by picking representatives that came closest to fitting his idea—and then he went further by faking the similarities.'"
John looked up from the book and said to Thomas, "It's the

third reason Wells gives that I find the most interesting. Listen to this."

John turned back to the book and read, "'Remember Darwin claimed that because the embryos are most similar in their early stages, this is evidence of common ancestry. He thought that the early stages showed what the common ancestor looked like—sort of like a fish. But embryologists talk about the developmental hourglass, which refers to the shape of an hourglass with its width representing the measure of difference. You see, vertebrate embryos start out looking very different in the early cell division stages. The cell divisions in a mammal, for example, are radically different from those in any of the other classes. There's no possible way you could mix them up. In fact, it's extremely different within classes. The patterns are all over the place. Then at midpoint—which is what Haeckel claimed in his drawings was the early stage—the embryos become more similar, though nowhere near as much as Haeckel claimed. Then they become very different again.'"

John looked up at Thomas and said, "Did you know these drawings were used as the main pieces of evidence in the court case to legalize abortion?"

Thomas's eyes widened and he exclaimed, "You mean to tell me that the courts used fraudulent evidence to legalize abortion?"

John simply nodded.

"How can that be? How could drawings, which were known to be fakes even in the days when they were first drawn, be admitted as evidence? That's just unbelievable."

John sat up a little, gave Thomas a quizzical look, and said, "You find it hard to believe that a liberal court would accept faulty evidence to advance their liberal agenda?" John shook his head.

Thomas stood up and paced behind his chair. Clearly agitated, he clenched his hands now and then as he thought about the full ramifications of what he just heard. Filled with frustration he said, "The courts are the ones we are supposed to depend upon for truth and justice!"

"Sit down, and I'll give you an example of the liberal court system's trustworthiness."

Thomas stopped pacing and slowly sat back down. He was not sure that he wanted to hear anything else that would upset him more than he already was. He held out some hope that he could believe in our court system.

"As you are aware, I was home schooled. My mother joined an organization called the Home School Legal Defense Association. They're a group of lawyers who provide protection to home schoolers from abusive school administrations and state or local authorities. Even though I'm no longer home schooled, my mom keeps up with her membership because she feels it's a worthwhile organization. Every month she gets a newsletter updating her on current events.

"One of the articles told how a family in Pennsylvania rushed their infant daughter to the hospital with breathing problems. The doctor in the emergency room wanted to start intravenous antibiotics and conduct a spinal tap. The quack didn't even give the child a thorough examination before wanting to start these procedures.

"The parents refused at first and asked the doctor to check her respiratory system. The doctor ignored their request and got the hospital's two social workers to help bully the parents into submitting to the procedures he prescribed. The parents finally consented. Later they found out that it was only a respiratory problem, as the parents predicted, and the infant needed only oxygen.

"But the social workers didn't stop there. They had a third social worker interrogate the parents about the doctor's allegations of 'possible medical neglect.' She drilled the parents at the hospital and wanted to look at the medical records of their other kids as well. The parents refused to show the social worker their kids' records.

"They called the Home School Legal Defense team, who told the social worker to back off because she had no legal grounds to pursue the matter. But the social worker ignored the warning and demanded to examine the family's home. At the advice of the Home School Legal Defense team, the parents refused this as well.

"One month later, in early March, the social worker petitioned the Susquehanna County Court to compel the parents to allow her to search their home. She had no evidence of wrongdoing, no probable cause. This social worker merely informed the courts that they had refused her a home visit. The court granted the social worker's request and mailed the parents an order giving them ten days to comply.

"Home School Legal Defense filed an appeal and petitioned for a stay of the order until the appeal was heard. The county court refused the petition for stay, as did the intermediate appellate court. The Home School Legal Defense Association then asked for a stay from the Pennsylvania Supreme Court. They refused as well. The social worker conducted her search and found absolutely nothing. No sign of wrongdoing. As far as I know the case is still up for appeal."

"If they had nothing to hide," Thomas asked, "why didn't they just let the social worker look inside their home?"

"You know, that is exactly what their friends and neighbors asked. Do you know what they told them?" Thomas just shook his head. "They told them it wasn't a matter of hiding something or not. The social worker had no reason to come into their home. That's what the Constitution is supposed to protect us from. Remember there was no evidence to support an affidavit for a warrant.

"Do you remember what the Fourth Amendment says? 'The right of the people to be secure in their persons, houses, papers, and effects, against unreasonable searches and seizures, shall not be violated, and no warrants shall issue, but upon probable cause, supported by oath or affirmation.' This court had no probable cause, yet it ordered the illegal search of that family's home. Nothing was found. It was totally bogus. Federal courts have ruled five times that social workers must have probable cause for a search.

"Can you think of any reason why a liberal court would have violated the Constitution in this way, Thomas, or why a liberal state Supreme Court would not issue a stay if there was a question of a constitutional violation?"

Thomas thought about it for a few seconds then said, "I didn't think they could legally do that."

"Legally they can't," John shot back, "but legally obviously means nothing to these liberal courts. They hold themselves above the law, that is the Constitution, and use the term unconstitutional as a talisman to promote their ideology. With what you have learned so far, can you guess why the liberal courts so aggressively went after this family?"

Thomas contemplated this. Obviously there was not enough evidence to show any form of medical mistreatment. The very fact that the family had brought the infant to the hospital at the first sign of trouble led proof to that. It sounded like the doctor felt chided by the parents' initial refusal of his recommended treatment and tried to exert his revenge through social services. With no evidence, there had to be some overriding factor for the court to pursue an

150

illegal action. John had mentioned, more than once, that the parents' legal counsel was from the Home School Legal Defense Association. With this in mind Thomas shrugged his shoulders and, more in the form of a question, said, "Because they were home schooled?"

"Yes, that is the basis. But why would the liberals attack home schoolers? Know this, through a number of tests, and with statistical evidence to back it, home schoolers have proven equal to and in many cases superior to their public school counterparts time and time again. So why the disdain?"

Thomas just shrugged.

"Let me give you a hint. You know I was home schooled. The curriculum I used explained that Haeckel's drawings were faked."

Thomas seemed puzzled for a few seconds, then the startled expression on his face told John that the light just turned on. Thomas said, "It's because they can't control what you learn! They can't indoctrinate you to their way of thinking. They lose control over you." Thomas paused as the reality of what he just said sank in.

"Bingo!" John said. "Now let's get back to our investigation about evolution."

"Okay," Thomas said, even though he felt his mind was in overload.

John looked back into the book. After a second or two he said, "Oh! Here is something interesting. Strobel wandered off the subject of Haeckel's drawings and asked Wells about gill slits in embryos. Strobel notes that *Life Magazine* in 1996, a liberal magazine I might add, described how human embryos grow, 'something very much like gills,' which the magazine claims is 'some of the most compelling evidence of evolution.'" As a way of example, John bent his head forward so that his chin touched his chest, just the way Wells had instructed Strobel to do, and asked Thomas, "Do you see these folds in my neck?"

"Yeah."

"Look, I've grown gills!" John said and chuckled.

Thomas squinted his eyes and asked, "You mean to say they are nothing more than folds of skin?"

"Wells said they're little more than that, but that they are definitely not gills. He added that even fish don't have gills at that stage of development. It's just evolutionists grasping at straws, trying to save a defunct theory. Don't you just love how accurate and reliable our liberal media is?" chided John. "Tom, do you remember earlier when we were discussing absolute truth? You asked the question why would liberals want to make people believe an opinion and the truth are the same?"

"Yeah, I remember. You said you would answer that question later. I guess that time has come."

"Yes," John said, "but I would like to see if you can answer the question yourself. Do you think you can?"

Thomas paused and stared at the table as he gave it some thought. Then he smiled and said, "Yeah, I think I can. If you can get the people to believe there is no absolute truth, and that one opinion is as good as the next, you don't have to come up with the facts or evidence to back your statement or belief. If someone challenges you to prove your opinion, you just call them a narrow-minded bigot and tell them they are too stupid to understand. That way the person backs off, and you, the liberal, can continue to promote your belief, even though there is no basis for it."

John was truly impressed. He just smiled and nodded. Then he said, "Let's move on to the last icon, shall we? Archaeopteryx (ar-key-OPT-er-icks)—the missing link. It's the cross between a bird and a lizard, right?"

Thomas raised his head a little and, planning not to commit to anything, said, "Well, that's what the media and our schools tell us."

"Yeah, that's what they tell us. But Wells explains they are not even close. Archaeopteryx is a bird. It has a bird's breeding system, bone structure, lungs, and distribution of weight and muscles. It's a bird. Wells also stated paleontologists agree that it's not even an ancestor of modern birds, but an extinct group of its own."

"But it looks so different from other birds."

"Wells compares the strangeness with that of the duck-billed platypus. Just a strange creature in a group by itself."

"So no missing link, huh?"

John shook his head and said, "No! No missing link. All so-called missing links have been either frauds or misrepresentations. Don't you find it amazing that when one of these fakes comes around, the press are all over it, wowing the world with the newest evidence of evolution? But when science finds out it's a fraud, you never hear about it. The press just can't seem to uncover that story."

Thomas didn't have a response. It's hard to realize that all, or too large a portion, of the knowledge you believed and the teachers you trusted to teach it, were fakes. Thomas just leaned back in his chair with his arms stretched out, hands pushing against the table.

John continued. "Strobel didn't just stop with Wells to show how evolution and Darwin's theory failed to amount to anything. He also interviewed top scientists from other disciplines as well. He interviewed professor of philosophy Stephen C. Meyer, cosmologist William Lane Craig, physicist Robin Collins, Professor J. P. Moreland, biochemist Michael J. Behe, and astronomers Guillermo Gonzalez and Jay Wesley Richards. In all of these sciences, as diverse as they are, the most modern discoveries all point strongly to intelligent design rather than random selection. Random selection just doesn't pan out. Most people believe that astronomy is the science that most supports life by chance; the odds are in its favor. I want to go over a little of what Gonzalez and Richards told Strobel. It's rather remarkable."

Thomas had relaxed again and was sitting in a half-slouched position. John saw that he was still attentive, so he explained in more detail. "Gonzalez and Richards first explained to Strobel about the Copernican Principle—that our planet is ordinary and that therefore life undoubtedly abounds in the universe. Let me read some of what Strobel wrote. 'Richards began, "We believe, however, that evidence is quite to the contrary." He gestured toward his colleague to continue. "We've found that our location in the universe, in our galaxy, in our solar system, as well as such things as the size and rotation of the Earth, the mass of the moon and so forth—a whole range of factors—conspire together in an amazing way to make Earth a habitable planet," Gonzalez said. "And even beyond that, we've found that the very same conditions that allow for intelligent life on Earth also make it strangely well-suited for viewing and analyzing the universe."

""And we suspect this is not an accident," Richards added. "In fact, we raise the question of whether the universe has been literally designed for discovery."' Richards and Gonzalez go on to explain why the rest of the universe is such an unlikely place for life to form. Quite simply there are too many dangers in space such as stars that supernova, hazardous giant molecular clouds, and black holes. They said that our spiral galaxy has safe zones between its arms where life can have a chance. But then you need just the right conditions in a solar system to help sustain life.

"You need the right size star. Too small and you produce too much radiation to sustain life; too large and the star dies before life develops. Then you need just the right planet configuration with an earthlike planet in just the right location with just the right size satellite to keep the planet's tilt in just the angle and so much more. When you put it all together, it is very likely that earth is the only planet in the universe that can sustain life. Only in TV science fiction shows can life be found on so many planets. There are more reasons why there should be no life in the universe than there are explanations how life started in the first place. All the evidence strongly suggests a creator and intelligent design rather than circumstance."

"Then why don't all scientists believe in God, and why isn't this being taught in schools?"

"You know, Tom, now you're thinking like an investigator," John smiled. "Why is an excellent question. Remember our hypothesis that liberals are a hate group? A hate group that hates God above all and then Christians. How would it benefit them by stifling and denying all the evidence of intelligent design and supporting and promoting falsehoods about evolution? Reason! Listen to a quote by Richard Dawkins, an Oxford evolutionist." John turned to the front of the book then read, "'The more you understand the significance of evolution, the more you are pushed away from an agnostic position and toward atheism.' So, Tom, if one philosophy leads you away from God and another philosophy confirms the existence of God, what are you going to do if you're a God hater?"

Thomas didn't even hesitate. "You are going to fight vigorously to prevent any of the evidence of God from getting to the public and demand that only what you want to believe is taught, regardless of how false it is."

"Exactly!" John smiled. "And if it is a hate group, we should be able to give examples where teachers or professors tried to bring out the evidence disputing evolution at prominently liberal institutions and have been chastised for it, right?"

Thomas nodded. Although he could not remember the details, he knew that such incidents had occurred recently at various schools. He even recalled that the issue had come up in the Kansas school system where parents wanted the evidence against evolution to be made known. The liberals had screamed bloody murder. Thomas was sure that John was going to give him clear examples where the liberal educators attacked some poor guy for speaking up, and he was right.

John returned Strobel's book to his backpack and pulled out *Persecution,* a book he had used earlier. Thomas had felt the title was a clue in their game. Now he knew that it was. John had told him that they were building a case against the liberal faction to show that they were a hate group similar to the Nazi party. In the same way that Hitler had planned the execution of Jews, John would show that liberals were planning the execution of Christians. His case seemed to be getting stronger and stronger by the minute.

John held up the book so Thomas could see the cover and said, "I have given you only a sparse number of instances where liberals have attacked and persecuted Christians. This book, by David Limbaugh, is a collection of hundreds of incidences exposing liberal bigotry. I want to read two incidences where professors were attacked because they spoke the truth about evolution."

John turned to a page he had marked and began to read, "'Speaking of academic freedom and tolerance, campus administrations around the country espouse it fervently but somehow cannot extend the principle to professors and others who courageously think outside the secular box. San Francisco State University took the position that a particular biology professor was no longer appropriate as a teacher of introductory biology. Professor Dean Kenyon, a leading national authority in chemical evolutionary theory, committed the unpardonable sin of exposing his students to certain points of dispute among scientists on macro-evolutionary theory. But worse, Kenyon reported the sacrilegious fact that a number of biologists admit to the existence of evidence for intelligent design in the universe.'"

John looked up to see if Thomas reacted to what he just read. Thomas just nodded, so John continued.

"'Similarly, Mississippi University for Women asked professor Nancy Bryson—the head of the school's Division of Science and Mathematics—to resign her position for exposing a group of honor students to scientific flaws in Darwinism taught in a presentation called "Critical Thinking on Evolution." The presentations covered alternative theories, including "intelligent design," and after the lecture a biology professor—who had not attended the talk—told Bryson that her talk was "religion masquerading as science." Bryson was incensed, saying, "The academy is all about free thought and academic freedom. He hadn't even heard my talk. Without knowing anything about my talk, he makes that decision. I think it's really an outrage." Encouraged by the outpouring of support from her students, Bryson refused to resign, whereupon school officials sent her a letter informing her they would not renew her contract in the fall as head of the division. After coming under heavy criticism, the university reversed itself, but Bryson hardly feels secure in her position. "I'm going to be watching my back," she said.'"

Thomas commented, "It sounds more like the Darwinists are practicing religion masquerading as science."

"I told you earlier that liberals attribute their own traits to others," John nodded.

He closed the book, put it on the table, then said, "You know, I picked up this book several times and have yet to finish it. After reading just a little about the various forms of open discrimination against Christians—or even as in the cases I just read where professionals are persecuted because they mention facts that lean toward the existence of God—I become so agitated that I can't read anymore. But I recommend this book and *A Case for a Creator* to any and all Christians who want to stay informed. I believe they should be required reading in Christian high schools.

"Anyway, let's look at these two incidents like detectives. We have two cases, both involving professors at universities. Both speak openly about the flaws of evolution. One is canned and the other is threatened with being canned. Do you know what the hypothesis for the scientific process is?"

"I think so," Thomas said. "All things are possible, but only some things are probable and must be determined by the facts available. Or pretty much like that. Is that what you're looking for?"

"Yes, that's pretty much it. Now with this description, and assuming that the instructors at these universities are supposed to be professors and scientists, would you say that the reactions of both university staffs were that of scientists?"

Thomas didn't have to think very hard on this one. "No, they were closed-minded, spiteful, and irrational."

"Would you say their reaction was more characteristic of a scientist or that of a religious zealot?"

Thomas gave this question a little more thought but not much more. "Their reactions were those of a religious zealot. It wasn't even close to being scientific or even professional."

"After what you've learned in Strobel's book, how would you assess the Darwin theory and those who follow it?"

Thomas needed to think about this question. He knew where John was going with this. Before he answered, he wanted to be sure he agreed. But as he reviewed everything he had learned so far that day, all the facts pointed to one logical conclusion. Anyway he himself had hinted at the answer just moments before.

He answered, "Although Darwin's theory was interesting, and at one time a viable hypothesis, the facts have rendered it obsolete. Therefore those who hold to its teaching do so not as scientists but as a cult. Those who are still believers of Darwinism do so because they have elevated Darwin's theory from science to a religion. They believe by faith alone."

John was impressed with his logical, precise answer. He always knew that Thomas was sharp. This made the game that much easier. Thomas had the reasoning ability that was the hallmark of a good detective. He might be able to get Thomas to change his major yet. He would do great in criminal justice.

"Very good!" John said. "Tell me, what issue has been the leading cause of wars over the past two thousand years?"

"Women!"

Both men laughed.

"I guess the right answer is religion," Thomas said.

"I think it probably is. And I won't tell Rebecca and the girls you said that." John got right back to business. He was anxious to be done by three o'clock, and he still had two other topics to cover. He asked, "Acknowledging that Darwinism or evolutionism or humanism, whatever they want to call their religion, is indeed a religion, why do you think there is so much animosity toward Christianity?"

"That's easy," Thomas said. "It's a rival religion with opposing views. One thing, John, nobody else recognizes it as a religion, so wouldn't this argument fall on deaf ears anywhere else?"

"True, this would fall on deaf ears in a court of law as it stands today. Although many prominent members in the Christian community have suggested that Darwinism is actually a religion, but they never seem willing to push the issue. Mostly this is for your benefit so you can see what Christians are up against, and to what extent liberals will be willing to go. You know what? I actually believe that liberals know that their faith in evolution is a religion, but as I've told you before this, liberals advance their cause by deceit and ignorance. They could never let the world know that evolution is just a religion or that would put them in jeopardy. They would lose the power they now have."

"How's that?"

"You remember the First Amendment to the Constitution? 'Congress shall make no law respecting an establishment of religion.' Well, that's exactly what the liberal Democrats and liberal judges have done. They have established evolution as the national religion. It's forced on American children in public schools and forced upon the public through liberal media. If you bring up creation, they scream separation of church and state. If it ever becomes well known and accepted that evolution is just another form of religion, then it too should fall under the separation of church and state ruling. I find it fascinating that all the other religions and religious philosophies are tolerated and taught in schools, but Christianity and the mention of the one true God is offensive to liberals."

"Why do you think that is?" asked Thomas. "Wouldn't you think they would bolt at any other competing religion?"

John shook his head and said, "Nah. Think about the psyche of a liberal. They want to be able to do anything they like and not be held responsible for their actions. So any religion that doesn't hold you to moral and ethical boundaries is just hunky dory with them. Remember they hate God because He gives us moral boundaries and plans to hold us accountable. This is why Darwinism or evolution or humanism is so appealing to them. If they can explain away God, they have no restraints. No matter how they hurt the next guy, it does not matter. They can't be held responsible for how they are!

"Now look on the other hand. If the evidence points to intelligent design, which it does, then there must be an Intelligent Designer—God. If God exists, and He is in contact with His creation, which He is, then there would be some kind of record by the persons He contacted. We call that record the Bible. Proof of that contact would be evident by the writings matching up with empirical science, which it does. Then logic would dictate that there is one true religion, that being Christianity. That explains their animosity toward Christians."

"What about the Jewish religion?" Thomas asked.

"The Jews are definitely God's chosen people. Christians are, in essence, an extension of that religion. For the Jews to remain faithful to their religion, however, they must deny the prophecies of their own prophets, which, in turn, means they deny God; therefore Judaism falls short of being the true religion. This does not mean they are no longer God's chosen people and that God hasn't made provisions for them."

John ended there, and Thomas sensed he didn't want to go any deeper into theology. At least not at this time. He thought about John's argument for about a minute, then simply said, "I agree."

John had glanced at his watch while waiting for Thomas to contemplate what he had said. It was nearly two o'clock. He felt he was making good time and would be done around three. He was thankful that Thomas had a good head on his shoulders and was making this easy.

John continued, "Good! Now I think it's time for me to show a parallel between modern liberals and Hitler's Third Reich. Tell me, do you think Hitler and his followers were evolutionists?"

Thomas leaned forward in his chair a little and said matter of factly, "Of course they were. That was their basis for the master race. They believed the Aryan race was the climax of the evolutionary process. This is why they felt no heartache at exterminating the so-called inferior races."

"Obviously you're well informed about that part of history, so I see no need to go over it. Let's look at the other similarities between liberals and the Nazi party. What do you know about Hitler's views about abortion?"

Thomas shrugged his shoulders slightly and said, "I really don't remember ever hearing anything about his views on the subject before!"

As John pulled out a piece of notebook paper with some handwritten notes on it, he said, "Probably not. Sam researched this subject for me and found only a little on it." John studied the paper for a minute. "This has some facts and a couple of quotes made by Hitler. Apparently, Hitler legalized abortion some time in 1933. By 1935, over 500,000 abortions were being performed in Germany each year. Strangely he and his party encouraged Aryan women to produce a lot of children but put the whole program into the hands of a decidedly pro-abortion medical establishment, kind of like our Planned Parenthood.

"In October 1941, the Nazi party decreed abortion on demand the official policy of Poland. Hitler, however, ordered that abortion be expanded to all populations under the control of the 'Ministry of the Occupied Territories of the East.' In 1942, Hitler is quoted saying, 'In view of the large families of the native populations, it could only suit us if girls and women there had as many abortions as possible.' He also said he would personally shoot any idiot who tried to forbid abortion in the occupied Eastern Territories. By the laws passed, the statistics, and the comments made by Hitler himself, it's pretty safe to say that he and his party were pro-abortion, especially when it came to what we would call the minorities.

"It's also common knowledge that the liberal Democrats have produced, sponsored, and pushed every piece of pro-abortion legislation from the sixties until present. It was our present conservative, Christian president that put an end to partial birth abortion. By the way, the liberals are fighting to make it legal again."

Thomas heard the passion in John's voice. His pitch was a little higher, his speech a little faster, and a touch of anger creased his eyes. Thomas continued to listen.

"I personally feel there are two reasons why liberals are such avid advocates for murdering our young."

Thomas interrupted in a mild manner, "Do you think murder might be too strong a term for this?"

John frowned at him, closed his eyes, and sighed.

"Some doctors say you can't even classify a fetus as human life," Thomas added.

CHAPTER 8

A MATTER OF ETHICS

J ohn silently stared into space for a couple of minutes. *Surely he's thinking about his response,* Thomas mused. Indeed John was. John had assumed that Thomas shared his views on abortion. Previously Thomas had commented that he was anti-abortion. He wondered if Thomas had taken that stance simply because his parents had. That was an OK reason for being against abortion—at least it steered you in the right direction. But John knew if a decision is not based on specific knowledge, a person can be easily persuaded to change his mind. John decided he needed to start with the basics.

Still focusing on nothing in particular, John said, "That's the problem with America today. People put too much faith in so-called experts. They never think things through for themselves."

Turning his attention toward his friend, he asked, "Thomas, what are the characteristics of life? Do you know the technical definition?"

"Not offhand, no."

John retrieved his dictionary, found the word life, and began to read, "'The quality manifested in functions such as metabolism, growth, response to stimulation, and reproduction, by which living organisms are distinguished from dead organisms or inanimate matter.' Tell me, Tom, is a paramecium a living organism?"

The question irritated Thomas a little. He thought that he had angered John, and now he was belittling him. But that just wasn't John. There had to be more to this. Thomas answered John's question to see what he was driving at. He simply said, "Yes."

"If scientists found a protozoan on Mars, even though it's a single cell, would they scream there's life on Mars?"

"Of course."

"So," John continued, "just because something is a single cell, its simplicity does not preclude it from being a life form, correct?" Thomas nodded. "Is a male sperm, even though it's only a single cell as it swims toward the ovum, a living cell?"

"Yes."

"Actually, Tom, it's not," John corrected him. "It's a manufactured cell that's not classified as living. It has no metabolism and it cannot grow or reproduce."

Thomas actually knew this, but he had answered too quickly to John's leading question. He half suspected John planned it that way.

"Is the ovum, prior to contact with male sperm, a living cell?" John asked.

Thomas was ready for this one. He was not going to give John just a yes or no answer this time. He was going to make sure that John knew he had some education. He answered, "No, like the sperm, the ovum is a manufactured cell. It's not until the first sperm pierces the membrane wall of the ovum that life begins. As soon as the ovum is pierced, its outer wall hardens to prevent any other sperm from piercing it. It then attaches itself to the uterus where it gets its nourishment and begins to grow."

"Very good. So we can say without any argument that life begins at conception, right?"

"Yeah," Thomas nodded. "I don't think there has ever been a question as to when life starts; just when doctors classify it as human."

"Okay," John said, "tell me, at conception, does that single cell contain the forty-six chromosomes necessary to develop human life?"

"Yes."

"Does it have a complete DNA code that would prevent it from becoming anything else? I mean, it couldn't become a lizard, could it?"

"No."

"How about a camel?"

"No."

"An eagle?"

"No."

"A palm tree?"

"No."

"A cactus?"

"Well, some women might say so at the time of birth."

John laughed out loud and Thomas joined him. The conversation seemed to be getting way too serious, and the joke helped to ease the tension.

"I'll have to give you that one," John said. "But in reality, scientifically, the only thing that single cell could turn into is a human being. All the genetic code, all the chemical makeup, everything that it takes to make a human being is in that one cell. So to call it anything other than human is preposterous. We established that life begins at conception. At that moment all the genetic and chemical codes point to the development of a human life. So the logical conclusion is that human life begins at conception."

It made sense to Thomas. He had never given it much thought before. He nodded his agreement to John, who continued, "You don't need to be a doctor or a rocket scientist to figure out something like this. With just a basic knowledge of biology and some common sense, we can repudiate the claim that a fetus isn't human life. Do you know the legal definition for murder?"

"Yes, I told you earlier today, remember? It's a willful killing of a human being with malice aforethought."

"Yeah, that's pretty much it. The overwhelming majority of abortions in the U.S. are for either the woman's convenience or the deadbeat father's convenience. Both the mother and doctor know they are intentionally killing the life within her. They have to schedule the execution of that human life. This legally constitutes malice aforethought. Therefore, Tom, abortion is just a passive term for murder. It's like killing one's wife and calling it divorce or killing an elected official and calling it impeachment. No matter what you call it, it's just plain murder—and it's wrong."

Thomas agreed with John. He couldn't believe he had ever thought there might be some justifications for abortion. Now he realized that was wrong. He asked, "Why would any doctor testify in court that an embryo wasn't a human being?"

"Two reasons—money and the liberal agenda." Thomas nodded his understanding.

"What's the most common reason liberals give for promoting abortion?"

Thomas thought a few seconds and said, "They say they are protecting a woman's right to choose."

"Yeah, a right to choose, my eye!" John grunted. "Any man who claims he wants to protect a woman's freedom of choice is lying. He's only interested in seeking his own pleasure. He doesn't want to be responsible for the financial burden and responsibilities of fatherhood in case he impregnates the woman he was with that week. And liberal women are so obnoxiously infected with male envy, they despise anything that emphasizes the difference between a man and a woman. And there is nothing like pregnancy to emphasize that difference."

While John stated his opinion, he reached for his copy of the Constitution. He handed it to Thomas and said, "Here, show me in the Constitution where a woman has the right to choose."

Thomas took the copy, looked at John, and shrugged. "I don't think I've ever seen or heard about that being written in the Constitution."

John took his copy of the Constitution back and said, "That's because it's not. You know, you hear a lot of people screaming about their constitutional rights, but they don't have a clue about what is actually written there. The Ninth Amendment deals with the rights of individuals not specifically protected by the Constitution. Let me read this to you, 'The enumeration in the Constitution, of certain rights, shall not be construed to deny or disparage others retained by the people.' Tell me, does that sound rather vague to you?"

"Yeah, it seems to leave it open to anyone's interpretation."

"Yeah, and that's the favorite argument of the liberal movement, but in reality, it's quite specific. It states that the government can't infringe on any other rights of the people. Let me make one thing perfectly clear—the government can't infringe upon our rights. The Constitution has no sway over the people nor can the government force it upon us, or at least it's not supposed to. This amendment protects our other rights."

John picked up his dictionary and quickly thumbed through it. He asked Thomas, "Do you know what a right is?"

Thomas had an idea, but it was obvious that John wanted an exact definition. He answered, "Go ahead and read it."

"'That which is just, morally good, legal, proper, or fitting.' If something is moral and ethical, then we have a right to do it. With every right come duties and obligations. You can't have one without the other. It just can't happen.

"But do you ever hear someone screaming about their duties and obligations? No way! Usually the people screaming about their rights do everything in their power to skirt their obligations. Just remind a liberal about his duties, and he will scream in your face, 'Don't push your morals on me!' It just doesn't work that way. Having rights without duties and obligations is called anarchy. No civilized society can tolerate that. Also when laws are passed, legitimate laws I mean, that restrict or monitor our rights, the laws should be directed to enforce the duties and obligations associated with those rights.

"Let's look at the right to choose. That is a God-given right. We do have freedom of choice, but the right is in the *ability* to choose. It does not mean that *what* we choose is a right. If you choose something that is unethical or immoral, you don't have a right to do it. It's absurd to think you should. A woman has the right to choose whether she wants to have sex or not. But with that right come duties and obligations. If she gets pregnant, then she has a moral obligation to that new life within her. That child needs to have the best chance at life that she can give it. If a woman doesn't want the responsibilities of motherhood and still has sex, then she needs to be smart enough to prevent a pregnancy from occurring. That is a duty associated with that right."

"That makes sense."

"I've got a question for you. Would smoking be a right?"

"No, it's a privilege," Thomas quickly answered. "A privilege is something that is not right but socially acceptable. They are also associated with duties and responsibilities."

"That's very good. Did you learn that in school?"

Thomas hesitated then said, "No, I heard it on the radio once. I don't remember why they were discussing it, but I do remember that part."

"A good part to remember. So logic and decency dictate that a woman has a right to choose what goes on with her body until she becomes responsible for a new life within her. Then moral obligations and duties kick in. So abortion is not a woman's right. Because it is not yet a practice generally accepted by all of society, so it can't even be considered a privilege. At best, it's a legal recourse granted by a corrupted court system. So what two overriding factors contribute to liberals being such staunch advocates of abortion?"

Thomas figured he had already heard John answer this question earlier. "For money and shedding parental responsibility," he responded.

"No, those are just liberal fringe benefits," John grinned. "The first reason is abortion numbs society to the horrors of mass murder. It strips away decency and morality and reduces human life to just innate objects. It also sets the next stage for the liberal's final solution."

Thomas looked bewildered, which made John grin again.

"Hitler started off with abortion in 1933. As soon as the German people were accustomed to that, on September 1, 1939, he gave Phillipp Bouhler and Dr. Karl Brandt, his assistants, the order to start a euthanasia program in which they targeted the elderly, mentally handicapped, and those with physical defects. An estimated fifty to sixty thousand German children and adults were killed by lethal injection or gassing between December 1939 and August 1941. From there it was a short step to Hitler's final solution, which we know as the Holocaust. Six million people killed because the people had been desensitized to murder.

"Did you know liberal doctors and psychologists have come up with a list of new terms to call groups of people they have classified as candidates for euthanasia? Do you know why they give these groups of people new terms to call them by?"

Thomas nodded and said, "It dehumanizes them."

"It's easier to kill someone you don't consider as human. And it makes it easier for the dim-wits of this world to buy. Liberals in America are pushing to institute euthanasia. With these liberal judges in place, it won't be long before one declares it constitutional."

Thomas shook his head in disgust and said, "I wish there was a way to get rid of these liberal judges!"

"There is," John said.

Thomas looked at John as if he was speaking Greek. He said, "I thought judges were appointed for life."

"Ah, but there is a condition," John said. Thomas looked at him intently as he quickly turned the pages to the Constitution. John said, "You remember we read in Article Two, Section Four of the Constitution that all civil officers shall be removed from office if convicted of treason, bribery, felonies, or even misdemeanors?"

"Yes, I remember that, but they haven't broken any laws."

"Well, none that we know of. An additional clause in Article Three, however, makes the judge's position the most tentative position in the government. The very first section of that article says, 'The judges, both of the supreme and inferior courts, shall hold their offices during good behavior.' If a judge is to keep his job during times of good behavior, that naturally implies that the antithesis is true—that they can be removed for bad behavior. Can you think of some things that might constitute bad behavior?"

Thomas pondered this and said, "Rendering too many bad judgments might be one."

"Actually that's a good one. If an appellate court over-turned a large number of decisions, that would show the judge is unfit for service. How about overstepping the authority of his bench? What if a judge declares someone in contempt of court, even when that person isn't involved with a trial or if there is no trial going on? Wouldn't you consider that bad behavior?"

Thomas was hesitant. "Give me an example."

"Okay, let's say court is in session. City workers are en-gaged in construction on the street below. The judge feels the noise is disrupting his court and issues a court order to stop the construction. Do you feel he has overstepped his authority?"

"Oh, yeah!" Thomas exclaimed. "Well over his author-ity. What the public is doing outside his courtroom is none of his business."

"I agree. What if a judge cites a person for contempt of court when there is no trial going on, but the person just didn't let the judge have his way in something totally unre-lated to a court case? Let's say a judge doesn't like the color of the curtains in his courtroom, so he asks the building manager to replace them. But, because of costs, the build-ing manager refuses, so the judge cites him for contempt of court. Would that be overstepping his authority?"

"Yes, most definitely. If a judge oversteps his authority, it should be classified as bad behavior."

"I agree with that too. How about if a judge hears a case outside his constitutional venue? What if he tries a case that the Constitution says is the responsibility of the state? Would that be bad behavior?"

"Yes, it would."

"How about if a judge makes such a bad ruling that he violates a citizen's rights or causes a public outcry? Would that be considered bad behavior?"

"Most definitely!"

"Okay! Then why didn't Congress remove the California judge who ruled that saying 'God' in the Pledge of Allegiance was unconstitutional? Why is he still on the bench? They all stood up and quoted the Pledge of Allegiance in defiance when they heard about it. Why didn't they go the extra step and call it what it was—bad behavior—and remove him?

"In Ex Parte McCardle, the Supreme Court recognized the power of Congress to deny the Court appellate jurisdiction in certain cases appealed from the circuit courts. After this tyranny, why didn't Congress pass an act prohibiting inferior courts from having the power to declare a law or anything, for that matter, unconstitutional? If a judge in one of the inferior courts feels there is justification to declare a law unconstitutional, then he should automatically appeal it to the Supreme Court where there are nine judges, not one. Otherwise you have a judicial dictatorship. This is the land of the free, not the land of tyrants. Why didn't Congress do this?"

Thomas shook his head. "I don't know," he said flatly.

"I'll tell you," John said. "It's one of two reasons. One, they are stupid and don't understand the Constitution or court precedence as well as they should. Two, they know they could and are practicing the good old boy system. Either reason is unacceptable."

174

Thomas thought about it for a moment or two. What John said made perfect sense. The scariest part was everything John had been saying up to now had made too much sense. Thomas had to admit that John's case—showing that liberals would someday soon commit genocide against Christians—was looking pretty strong. His curiosity got to him. John had said the liberals were pushing abortion for two reasons.

"John, what's the second reason liberals are pushing abortion?"

"I thought you'd never ask! This is strictly my opinion, and there is no direct proof as far as I know. I believe it's for religious purposes—ritual human sacrifice."

"What!" Thomas exclaimed loudly. "Are you nuts? How did you ever come up with that one?"

John smiled. The look on Thomas's face was comical. John replied, "Remember I told you this is just an opinion. You know about opinions, don't you?"

"I've herd the adage. Opinions are like..."

"Yep, thats the one." John interrupted. "All kidding aside, I don't think this is too far-fetched. I'm looking at the big picture, the liberal society as a whole. Remember how we noted that their devotion to evolution is akin to religious zeal? Their emotional response to anything that would stop abortion is abnormal as well. Remember how I said history has a way of repeating itself?" Thomas nodded, so John went on. "Well, every aspect of the liberal mind-set and culture directly parallels Baal and Asherah worship."

"I've heard of that before, but I can't place where."

"It's in the Bible. The people living in Canaan worshiped these gods. Their cult was based on sex, self-gratification, and self-interest. They also burned their babies on the altar as sacrifices to Baal and Asherah. Men and women who didn't want to be inconvenienced with the responsibilities of parenthood gave their children to the high priests for slaughter. I find it remarkable how today's liberals zealously advocate partial birth abortion. There's no way you could mistake the victim for anything other than human. Like the people living in Canaan, Hitler was a pagan too."

"Is there any evidence of this that you would be able to present in a court of law?"

"Nah! This is just food for thought. An idea to share with friends."

"You know, John, all this talk about euthanasia reminds me of the death class* we had back at Columbine."

"What kind of class?" John shot a puzzled look at Thomas.

"Our death class. One of the teachers counseled us that, if we had problems that we thought were too great for us to handle, suicide was a viable option. They even taught that by committing suicide we were doing the community a service."

John wore a look of total disbelief. Thomas had said every word with a straight face. He was obviously telling the truth, yet John still asked, "Are you kidding me?"

"No, I'm serious! They said that it was actually a good thing for us to kill ourselves."

"What did your parents say about that?"

"I never told them. The instructor told us that this was something we weren't supposed to share with them. Now it seems kind of foolish to have obeyed that order."

"No doubt," said John. His contempt for the public education system just increased tenfold. "Did they teach that class at the time of the massacre?"

"I don't know, but it makes you think, doesn't it?"

---

*David Limbaugh, *Persecution* (Washington, DC: Regnary Publishing Inc., 2003), 84.

"Yes, it does. I have some more food for thought I'd like to dish out. Do you notice that liberals are screaming bloody murder about President Bush's decision to ban embryologic stem cell research? Even though adult stem cells and placenta stem cells do everything that embryologic stem cells are expected to do, liberals want to utilize only the stem cells that take a human life—the means by which they can kill something.

"Did you know that Nazi doctors conducted medical experiments on Jewish prisoners in the concentration camps? Doctors watched as victims froze to death. Most of what we know about hypothermia came from those experiments. Although we gained a wealth of information from these experiments, that still does not make it right.

"Although Hitler didn't prohibit Aryan women from getting abortions, his main desire was for minorities to have them. Did you know that the vast majority of abortions conducted today are performed on minorities? Liberals in California have even solicited the aid of a Hispanic who calls himself a cleric to persuade the Hispanic population to have more abortions. I guess the liberals feel there are just too many of those people around. Just something to chew on.

"Oh! One more thing before we move on to the last subject. Have you ever noticed how liberals, especially liberal talk show hosts, have the recurring theme that whites should help the black people? It's a subtle way to insinuate that blacks are inferior—the same agenda propagated by Hitler and his Nazi Party. Something to ponder."

John saw Thomas was thinking about the implications of what he just said. He gave him a minute without responding before he moved on to the last topic for the day.

"Let's discuss the last parallel of the liberals of today and the Nazi party of old. I think it's pretty common knowledge that liberal politicians constantly submit bills into legislation proposing the ban of, or the registration of, guns in America. This is clearly in violation of the Second Amendment. 'A well regulated Militia, being necessary to the security of a free state, the right of the people to keep and bear arms, shall not be infringed.' So why are liberal politicians so desperate to enact gun control laws? An example would be the Brady Bill. By the way, did you know that it's supposed to expire some time this year?"

"No, I really hadn't followed it too closely," Thomas admitted.

"Yeah, that was just some gee wiz information anyway. You know I like to hunt. The March 2004 issue of *American Hunter* published an article titled 'The Bias against Guns.' The author, John R. Lott Jr., points out that there are four times as many instances where citizens use firearms to defend themselves against criminals than there are instances where a citizen is harmed by a gun accidentally. Yet the liberal press almost never report a time where someone saves his own life or the life of another using a gun. It's pretty much guaranteed that they will report someone being victimized by a gun. That is censorship—the media relaying only the facts they want you to know. Do you know why they do that?"

"Yep. By not keeping us fully informed, they can manipulate the people to share their point of view. Limited knowledge means uninformed decisions."

"Excellent!" John said. "Like I mentioned earlier, I would rather have the government censoring what we saw rather than the press themselves. At least that way you know what you're looking at is suspect. When the press censors, you never know what is a lie or the truth. So why are liberal politicians and the liberal media collaborating in an effort to establish gun control?"

John pulled out another article from his backpack and placed it on the table before him. Thomas easily read the large, bold print. "Registration: The Nazi Paradigm."

"I have some idea," Thomas said, "but I'm sure I'll have a clearer idea after we review that."

John smiled. Thomas was a fast learner. "Yeah, I think you'll find this fascinating. I found this article by Stephen P. Halbrook, PhD, JD, covering Hitler's gun control policy. I want to read a couple of passages that will make it clear why liberals are so big on gun control.

"'Himmler, head of the Nazi terror police, would become an architect of the Holocaust, which consumed six million Jews. It was self-evident that the Jews must be disarmed before the extermination could begin. Finding out which Jews had firearms was not too difficult. The liberal Weiman Republic passed a Firearm Law in 1928 requiring extensive police records on gun owners. Hitler signed a further gun control law in early 1938. Other European countries also had laws requiring police records to be kept on persons who possessed firearms. When the Nazis took over Czechoslovakia and Poland in 1939, it was a simple matter to identify gun owners. Many of them disappeared in the middle of the night along with political opponents.'

"I also want to read a quote from Hitler that's not in Halbrook's articles. 'The most foolish mistake we could possibly make would be to allow the subject races to possess arms. History shows that all conquerors who have allowed their subject races to carry arms have prepared their own downfall by so doing. Indeed, I would go so far as to say that the supply of arms to the underdogs is a *sine qua non* for the overthrow of any sovereignty. So let's not have any native militia or native police. German troops alone will bear the sole responsibility for the maintenance of law and order throughout the occupied Russian territories, and a system of military strong-points must be evolved to cover the entire occupied country.' You know, Hitler learned from history. Why can't we?"

John didn't expect an answer so he continued after a slight shrug from Thomas. "I have some more passages I want to read from Halbrook's article. 'In 1941, U.S. Attorney General Robert Jackson called on Congress to enact national registration of all firearms.' I want you to notice, Tom, that Jackson was a political appointee of Franklin D. Roosevelt—the architect of today's liberal Democratic party."

Thomas heard the disdain in John's voice as he said Democratic and interrupted, saying, "Come on, John. Call them the communist party. You know you want to."

"At least it would be a truer depiction. Let me read. 'Given events in Europe, Congress recoiled, and legislation was introduced to protect the Second Amendment. Republican Edwin Arthur Hall explained: "Before the advent of Hitler or Stalin, who took power from the German and Russian people, measures were thrust upon the free legislatures of those countries to deprive the people of the possession and use of firearms, so that they could not resist the encroachments of such diabolical and vitriolic state police organizations as the Gestapo, the Ogpu, and the Cheka." Republican John W. Patman added: "The people have a right to keep arms; therefore, if we should have some Executive who attempted to set himself up as a dictator or king, the people can organize themselves together and with the arms and ammunition they have, they can properly protect themselves."'

"I want to read just a few more passages. 'Switzerland was the only country in Europe, indeed in the world, where every man had a military rifle in his home. Nazi invasion plans acknowledged the dissuasive nature of this armed populace.' Tom, Germany never invaded Switzerland. I want to read part of his closing paragraph. 'Schemes to confiscate firearms kept by peaceable citizens have historically been associated with some of the world's most insidious tyrannies.'

"I looked on the net too for examples of these tyrannies and found this list: 'In 1911, Turkey established gun control. From 1915 to 1917, 1.5 million Armenians, unable to defend themselves, were rounded up and exterminated.

"'In 1929, the Soviet Union established gun control. From 1929 to 1953, approximately 20 million dissidents, unable to defend themselves, were rounded up and exterminated.

"'In 1935, China established gun control. From 1948 to 1952, 20 million political dissidents, unable to defend themselves, were rounded up and exterminated.

"'In 1938, Germany established gun control. From 1939 to 1945, 13 million Jews, gypsies, homosexuals, the mentally ill, and political dissidents, who were unable to defend themselves, were rounded up and exterminated.

"'In 1956, Cambodia established gun control. From 1975 to 1977, one million "educated" people, unable to defend themselves, were rounded up and exterminated.

"'In 1964, Guatemala established gun control. From 1964 to 1981, 100,000 Mayan Indians, unable to defend themselves, were rounded up and exterminated.

"'In 1970, Uganda established gun control. From 1971 to 1979, 300,000 Christians, unable to defend themselves, were rounded up and exterminated.'

"The liberals know from history that before it's safe to exterminate Christians, they have to take away our guns. America, for the time being, is the last free country in the world, the last safe haven for Christians. Before the liberals can safely make their move to the final solution, America's freedom must crumble altogether. That won't happen while we maintain our right to keep and bear arms."

Thomas caught a subtle hint that John was not just talking about liberal Democrats here in the U.S. He asked, "You said before liberals can safely make their move, America's freedom must crumble. Are you including liberals outside the U.S. as well?"

"Yes, I am. If you have ever listened to the policies and goals of the U.N., you know that there is no difference in ideology. The liberal's goals are the same throughout the world."

"Do they call themselves liberals in other parts of the world?"

"Yes, like the U.S., world politics are marked with conservative, liberal, and moderate factions. The vast majority of nations have openly adopted socialism. In many places such as Britain, Canada, Australia, and Brazil, the government loosely holds the reins, but the people are definitely bridled. Here in America we still spit out the bit, but we're not putting up as much of a fight as in the past. Do you know who started the U.N.?"

Thomas shook his head no.

"Franklin D. Roosevelt and his wife Eleanor—the first directors, the masterminds, and the most infamous founders of the liberal Democrat or 'communist' party—also spearheaded the U.N. Is there any need to question why the philosophies are the same? It's because the architect is the same."

Thomas nodded his understanding then asked, "So America's involvement in the U.N. is actually a bad thing?"

"Yes. We don't have time for an in-depth study of political science, but let me say this. If America submits itself to U.N. authority, America will lose its sovereignty. We will all become slaves. Perhaps I should use the more appropriate, politically correct term—peasants." John watched as Thomas thought about all that was said. He had fed Thomas a lot of information. Now it was time to see if he had made a strong enough case that Thomas would feel confident taking it before a court.

"Tom, I've given you a brief description on how America was founded on Christian principles and beliefs and that God is very much part of the workings of our society. I have shown you how the philosophies of the liberals and the Nazi party under Adolf Hitler parallel each other. This includes their support of abortion, evolution, gun control, and homosexuality. You've probably figured out when we quit using biblical terminology in the dictionary. I've given you examples of discrimination against Christians and examples of government abuses. I just scratched the surface of every subject. By no means have I gone into the detail that I could have with any these subjects. If I tried to cover it all, it would easily take two semesters." John paused and looked almost startled.

"I almost forgot. There is one more parallel between these two groups that I need to emphasize. Have you ever noticed how the liberals do everything they can to demonize Christians today? Hitler did the same to the Jews. Hitler and the Nazis compared the Jews with being rats. The Nazis accused the Jews of being low-lifes who stripped the German people of their jobs and their rightful riches—this coming from socialists. Today's liberals call Christians hate-filled bigots who have no tolerance; therefore, we should not be tolerated. The hypocrites! They use reverse psychology. Like I told you earlier, liberals always apply their own characteristics to those they hate. They promote and exalt the writings of any Christian-hating author such as Friedrich Nietzsche."

"I've heard of Nietzsche," Thomas interrupted. "Phil read his stuff to us in class. He said Nietzsche was one of the greatest philosophers of our time."

"Phil said that, did he? Go figure," John replied. "For the simple-minded I guess he probably is a great philosopher. Let's look at Nietzsche's writings and determine if he is a great philosopher or just a Christian-hating bigot. Do you remember how Nietzsche starts out his writings?"

"Vaguely. I believe he starts out by calling Christians fools."

"That's right. Nietzsche starts out with a Christian running from place to place as if he's lost and dejected, asking those he encounters if they found Christ. Those people mock him, saying, 'Have you lost him, is he in hiding, has he run away?' I can't remember the exact wording. Do you know why he starts out mocking and belittling Christians?" Thomas just shook his head, so John answered his own question.

"Intimidation. He knew that the weak-minded and Christians weak in faith would buckle under the onslaught of ridicule. People hate the thought of looking stupid and bolt from anything that may be associated with stupidity. By starting with name calling, he knew that the weak-minded and the weak in faith would disassociate themselves from the object of stupidity—by his reckoning, Christianity. He also knew that would open their minds to his subsequent hate-filled preaching. Tom, what are the two traits that liberals use to advance their cause?"

"Ignorance and deceit."

"That's right. Did you know that Nietzsche's father and grandfather were preachers?"

"Yes, I did. Phil mentioned it. He said that's how Nietzsche was educated enough to see the mythology of Christianity and become the great philosopher that he was."

John just shook his head. He knew if a teacher ridiculed any other religion, the school system would have given him the boot. "Well, Nietzsche lied. He knew enough about Christianity to know that when a Christian asks a person if he has found Jesus, it wasn't because the Christian was looking for him. He knew that the Christian already had a relationship with Christ. Nietzsche knew that the believer was inquiring to see if that person has been informed about Christ. He twisted this fact to belittle Christians and ultimately God. Nietzsche claims to be an atheist. How can we tell that's a lie as well?"

Thomas just shrugged his shoulders.

"In his writings he claims to have murdered God. Why would you murder someone you didn't believe in? More than that, to him it's through murder that the human race is elevated to the equivalence of God, giving us the ability to do what we please, free from guilt. Nietzsche also questioned our service to God. He asked, 'Why should we serve God?' If he doesn't believe in God, why would the question of service ever come up? Nobody even thinks about serving something they don't believe in.

"When you examine Nietzsche's writings, anyone with a brain can deduce that he was nothing more than a recalcitrant little boy who hated his heavenly Father. Can you guess what caused such adamant hatred in him?"

Thomas thought back to what Phil had taught him. He just could not remember all that much. He recalled the things that John talked about as he mentioned them, but a reason for such abhorrence eluded him. Finally he said, "I can't even begin to guess."

"Let me give you a hint. The number one trait of a liberal is perversity, especially sexual perversity."

Thomas squinted his eyes as he guessed, "He was a homosexual?"

185

"No, he wasn't a homosexual. He wanted to commit incest. He wanted to take his sister as a lover."

"Oh, that's disgusting!" Thomas exclaimed.

"Yes, it is," John agreed. "He was denied his forbidden love because of the commands of God, therefore he chose to hate and, in his mind, kill God. A great philosopher? No way! A talented and gifted writer, most definitely. But he was too hateful to be a great philosopher."

"It makes you think less of the science of philosophy, doesn't it?"

"Philosophy is just the opinion of others. I never did put much stock in it. Now, with what you have been given, do you think we would have built a clear enough case to show that liberals are planning and working their way toward the extermination of the Christian faith? Would you be willing to present this in a court of law?"

Thomas paused before he answered. "John, I'm just not sure. You've given me so much information. I just need time to think about it."

"That's fair. And really, Tom, that is the whole purpose behind this game. It's to get people to start thinking. If they don't agree, at least they can see that more goes on than meets the eye. People have become so complacent these days, we just need a wake-up call. But whatever you believe, Tom, I want it to be because you have thought it through and did not rely on another to make up your mind for you. That's the important thing."

"You've done this with the others as well, haven't you?"

"Yes. First with Paul. After speaking with Sam, I tweaked it some. Then I met with Rebecca and Tami together. Still some more tweaking after that."

"Probably some more tweaking after today, huh?"

"Yeah, a little more," John smiled.

186

"Did the others accept your analogy?"

"Paul and Rebecca did. Tami refused to believe that anything like the Holocaust could happen here in America."

"Yeah, it's a pretty scary thought. Let's say you're right. Should we be preparing for war or something?"

John grimaced slightly. *Why does it seem that everyone's first solution to a problem is war?* After the loss of his brother, the thought of war left a bad taste in John's mouth. Yet John was wise enough to know you could not abandon that solution altogether.

"The Declaration of Independence says, 'But when a long train of abuses and usurpations, pursuing invariably the same object evinces a design to reduce them under absolute Despotism, it is their right, it is their duty, to throw off such Governments, and to provide new Guards for their future security.' So war is a viable course of action. However, and I want to emphasize this, it should always be the last course and used only when all other intelligent options have been exhausted. I truly believe that it will never come to that. If we can just educate people, we can vote in new leaders who will bring us back to being the great, God-fearing nation we once were."

"Could the liberals take any actions that would indicate that open warfare was the only solution?"

John stared into space, deep in thought.

"Yes, I can think of three instances that would indicate that the American people should take up arms. First, if the people in a free election vote by majority to pass a law and then the government refuses to enact it, depending on the law, the people would be justified to take up arms. Second, if foreign troops are ever used here in America as a means to police the public. Hitler moved troops who lived in one region to police the people of a different region of Germany. In this way there were no ties, no relations between the troops and the citizens. Hitler knew it was much easier for people to carry out acts of brutality on people you didn't know. So if our government ever incorporates foreign troops to police us, you can be sure our rights are going to be stripped from us. Expect some rough treatment. Third, if the government ever passed a law to take away our guns or, for that matter, forced us to register our guns, this would be a total violation of our Second Amendment rights. It's also a sure sign for Christians that their slaughter is near at hand. I would say these are three legitimate reasons why people would forgo the peaceful, more intelligent route of cleaning up our government."

"What if the government passed a new amendment that repeals the Second Amendment?"

"They can't," John said. "The Bill of Rights contains protective clauses designed to shield the people from government abuses. There are other protective clauses in the Constitution as well. If the federal government, or any one of the governments, could arbitrarily repeal those protections, what kind of protection would they be?"

Thomas nodded his head in understanding and said, "They would be no protection at all."

"That's right. For all intents and purposes we should consider these protective clauses as written in stone, and no government entity would have the means to revoke them. If they did, that would be the fourth legitimate reason for the people to go to war. Still I prefer educating the people and using peaceful means."

"Maybe you should write a book," Thomas chided.

"Nah, in today's culture you'd have to make it into a movie or no one would ever hear about it."

CHAPTER 9

REVELATION

J ohn looked at his watch, three-twenty. "Are you ready
to go?" John asked.

"Sure," Thomas replied. John gathered all of his paper-
work and books and stuffed them in his backpack, then they
headed for the door. Thomas held the door open for John.
As he walked through, Thomas commented, "So you must
be a staunch Republican then."

John waited for Thomas to catch up with him to reply.

"No, I don't like the Republican party either. They're
too compromising and gutless and probably just as corrupt.
I'm willing to bet liberal conspirators are within their ranks.
Infiltrate, disrupt, and destroy. Any good general would do
it. It's being done to the Church. Even Jesus warned against
false teachers and wolves dressed in shepherd's clothing.

"Actually, I'm an independent. I don't think the populous should affiliate itself with a particular party. Remember
when we discussed your mother being a Democrat? People
feel they have to be loyal regardless if they agree with the
party or not. As an independent one is free to think for

himself, find the candidate he agrees with the most, and vote for him. Party membership should be left for those aspiring to be politicians."

"Whom do you plan to vote for then?" Thomas asked, panting. John walked quickly as he talked.

"Bush, although I would truly like to vote for the candidate in the Constitutionalist party. Not enough people know about that party and what they truly represent to reasonably believe he has a chance. Most people mistakenly believe that the Constitutionalist party is run by a bunch of militia nut cases. Liberals promote this view even though it's far from the truth. The liberals definitely don't want the government to be restricted by the Constitution, so they will do anything to make this party look bad.

"Voting for Bush helps keep Kerry out of office. I think Kerry would be a far worse president than Clinton was, if possible. Although I don't think Bush is a great choice, he is a better choice by far of the two."

Thomas fell silent for a couple of minutes while he thought about that. Then he asked, "Doesn't the Bible predict something about worldwide persecution of Christians?"

"Yep," John said. "You can find that in Revelation 6:9 and 12:17."

John didn't say anything else so Thomas asked, "Won't Christians be raptured by then?"

John immediately stopped and asked, "You know about the pre-tribulation rapture theory?" A shocked expression crossed his face.

"Well, yeah! I am a Christian." Thomas was a little miffed.

John nodded once in concession. "It's just that I've sometimes wondered about the validity of your faith. I'm not trying to be mean. It's just that sometimes you don't seem to take your faith too seriously, you have to admit."

"Well, I am," Thomas retorted.

"Good," John said with a warm smile, "then I can take you off my prayer list. To answer your question, I don't believe in a pre-tribulation rapture."

Now Thomas looked shocked. He thought all Christians believed in a pre-tribulation rapture. He asked, "You don't? Why?"

"Because the Bible says there won't be one."

"But all the big-name ministers preach about it. How could they be wrong?"

"I know they do, but all the passages they use to support their theory are about *how* it will happen, not *when*. Read Matthew 24:15, Mark 13:14, and especially 2 Thessalonians 2:1–4. Then read Daniel 12:11. Decide for yourself when the rapture can occur. Many preachers say the tribulation is a time of God's wrath, and Christians are not meant to suffer that wrath. I agree, but Revelation 14:12 says, 'This calls for patient endurance on the part of the saints who obey God's commandments and remain faithful to Jesus.' It's talking about the saints who don't take the mark of the beast during the tribulation.

"Psalm 11 says God tests the righteous and the guilty alike. Didn't God test Job, Abraham, and Moses, all considered righteous in God's eyes? Look at God's example of the Church—the Hebrews rescued out of Egypt. Didn't He test them for forty years in the desert? I think it's absurd to think that God won't test us at least one more time." John glanced at his watch and said, "Tom, I've got to run if I plan to get to the store and back in time to go out. I'll see you back at St. Charles Hall about fivish, OK?"

"Oh, yeah. Sure, see you then."

"Bye."

Thomas stood there for a few seconds thinking about the events of the day. He noticed that they had stopped in front of the centerpiece for the school—a statue of Mary, the mother of Jesus. She held Jesus as a small child in her hands. Jesus stood with His arms spread wide like they would be when He was nailed to the cross.

As Thomas pondered the statue, his mind drifted to the movie, *The Passion of the Christ*. The press had made such a big deal out of the showing. They had called it a hate film. They claimed it would stir anti-Semitic feelings, more hatred for the Jews. Thomas recalled that Mel Gibson and Jim Caviezel had received death threats. Then all at once it dawned on him. *The Passion of the Christ* did stir up hatred. The hatred of the liberal press and liberals in general for Christians.

John had been right. Everything he said fell into place. Thomas was sure of it now. The liberals were planning to exterminate Christianity even if it meant genocide. A rush of emotions coursed through his body. Externally it must have looked like pain. Thomas hadn't noticed the three girls who walked past, but one of them called out, "Thomas, are you all right?"

Thomas didn't know two of them, but the girl who called out was Joy, a student in his Algebra 1 class. She was a plain-looking girl who always wore black, thick-rimmed glasses. She never wore makeup as far as he could tell, kept her brown hair in a bun on top of her head, and always wore baggy clothes. Thomas was sure she had worn that same sweatshirt everyday in class. He assumed she wore it because she was overweight. Still, she always had been nice to him. He had borrowed a pencil from her on a few occasions, and she had asked him for paper from time to time. But at most they had polite conversations. She just wasn't Thomas's type.

Awkwardly he said, "Yes, I was just standing here thinking about *The Passion of the Christ*, the movie."

"Why, Thomas, are you giving yourself to Christ?" Joy asked.

Thomas considered her question. After what he had learned, he felt it was time to become more serious about his faith. Why shouldn't he devote his life to Christ? Look what He had done for him. Look at the promise he had in Him.

"Yes, I am!" he answered Joy.

"Oh, Thomas!" she exclaimed. "I've prayed that you would."

Why did she think I needed prayer for coming to Christ? He frowned and asked, "You've prayed for me?"

"Well, yes," Joy nervously responded. She felt like a child who got caught with her hand in the cookie jar. "You've always been so kind to me in math, and it wasn't apparent that you had Christ in your life." Joy noticed the shocked expression that crossed his face. *Oh, what a cruel thing to say,* she thought to herself. *I could just die!* She knew then if she ever had a chance to be with him, she had just blown it for good. She said, "I'm sorry, I didn't mean..."

"No, that's okay!" interrupted Thomas.

She was the second person in ten minutes to tell him that it was not evident that he was a Christian and that they had prayed for him. What had they seen? What *hadn't* they seen? He didn't feel he was any different from anyone else in the world.

Then it occurred to him. His pastor had taught him that Christians were not of the world but should be a light upon it. Thomas had always thought of himself as a Christian, always said he was a Christian, but acted just like his old friends who were not. He was like everyone in the world.

After what he had just learned, that thought actually made him queasy.

Thomas noticed that Joy looked as if she had just lost a dear pet. Her shoulders drooped a little, and what he could see of her eyes, behind those thick-rimmed glasses, looked sad. He felt compassion and was actually touched that she had taken the time to pray for him.

Out of compulsion he said, "A group of my friends and I are going to dinner and taking in a movie. Would you be willing to accompany me?"

In an instant her shoulders squared and her eyes brightened. For the first time Thomas noticed they were brown. Her cheeks were naturally rosy with a light sprinkling of freckles. Her lips were full and slightly redder than most. It was a nice trait. He could see now that she wasn't wearing any makeup. Her lips widened into a smile as she said, "Yes, I'd like that."

"Great," Thomas said. "I'll pick you up at your dorm around five. We're going to meet at St. Charles Hall at about five-fifteen to five-thirty. We usually decide then where we're going to eat."

"That's fine. I'm in Guadalupe Hall, room 221."

"OK," Thomas said. "I'll see you then."

"I'll see you then."

"Bye," Thomas said as he turned and made his way toward Benton Avenue. As Joy and her friends walked to their dorm, she turned to see if Thomas was watching. He wasn't. She grabbed a hand of each friend, squeezed, and said, "He asked me out!"

As Thomas entered his home, he found his roommate, Sam Stein, reclined on the easy chair with the newspaper propped in front of him. As Thomas walked into the sparsely decorated room, Sam peeked over the paper and asked, "How'd it go?"

Thomas looked at his watch. "Oh, from about six-thirty to three-thirty," Thomas said in a serious manner.

"You smart alec," Sam rebuffed. "How did you like the lesson?"

"As a game, it wasn't much fun, but as a lesson, it was great. And I have to admit, a little scary. John's not very politically correct is he?"

Just the day before, Sam had talked with John about addressing political correctness and the liberals' use of it. Sam felt John should tackle the issue and expose its negative effects. John felt it was a good idea but wanted to hold off until he could do some research. He wanted to find some real-life examples to back up their opinion. John had decided not to broach the subject during his encounter with Thomas that day.

John always liked to be thorough in investigating facts before implementing them in his narration. Sam, on the other hand, did not mind sharing his opinion even if he did not have specific evidence on hand to back what he was saying. He believed people should be given the opportunity to hear what you had to say, and then seek out the evidence for themselves if they were so inclined. Sam's answer was a little more than the simple bantering back and forth that Thomas meant to engage in.

"No, he's not, but there's a good reason for that. Have you ever noticed how political correctness crept into our culture in just the past couple of decades? At one time you could speak the truth about somebody, and if he took offense, it was his problem. It just meant he needed to change his ways. But then the liberals introduced political correctness—so-called polite talk that would prevent anyone from being offended. Good ploy, but the liberals don't practice what they preach, do they?"

"No, they don't. There is no moratorium on offending a Christian. Actually it seems that type of offending is politically correct."

Sam nodded. "So then, you see their strategy?"

Thomas squinted his brows to form a quizzical look upon his face. He inquired, "Strategy?"

Sam answered, "Political correctness is just a subversive form of mind control, used to manipulate the simpletons of this world. First the liberals started out by insisting we change some common terminology to less offensive language. For example, not saying handicapped and saying physically disabled instead. Not that anyone was ever offended by the term handicapped or any other of the common terms in the first place. But if you are going to practice mind control, you have to start somewhere. It's always best to start with the basics. Tell someone they should be offended by a term, and they will be offended.

"After a continual bombardment of being told we have to be more politically correct, people began to conform to this new politeness. It was bogus, but it served their purpose. Then they conned people into believing that we should never speak the truth about something if it might hurt someone's feelings. First it was suggested that we not push our individual morals on someone else, as if morals are an individual preference, then they demanded it. From there they brainwashed us to believe that we must tolerate all types of behavior. We are no longer merely to refrain from rebuking someone from doing what is wrong, but now we have to accept their wrongdoing as if it were right. If we don't accept this wrong or alternative behavior, we are intolerant and the ones in the wrong. They use this philosophy as leverage against Christians in court. The Bible predicted that people would make what is wrong, right and what is right, wrong. It's mindless stuff when you know what to look for, but it seems that liberals have dulled the minds of Americans so much over the past two decades that few people today know what to look for."

"That's why John kept repeating that the liberal's best weapons were ignorance and deceit."

"That's right," Sam said. "That's why John and I, and hopefully you, won't ever be politically correct. Sometimes people just need to hear the truth. If it offends them, oh well!"

"Do you believe as John does that within ten years, if things stay the same, Christians will be rounded up for the slaughter?"

"Yeah, Tom, I do. Personally I think it will be less than ten."

"What can we do?" Thomas asked.

Sam shrugged his big shoulders and said, "I guess the best thing for us to do is pray people open their eyes and get off their butts."

Thomas nodded and then said, "I rededicated my life to Jesus today."

Sam dropped the paper and bolted out of his seat. "You did, really? That's great, Tom! Did you and John pray together?"

"No," Thomas said, "it happened after we went our separate ways."

"Would you like me to pray over you?" Sam asked.

"Well, sure," Thomas hesitated. He knew that Sam went to a charismatic church and wasn't too sure what to expect.

Sam placed both his hands on Thomas's shoulders, bowed his head, and prayed, "Heavenly Father, we thank You for bringing this sheep back into the fold, for the church is blessed by this addition. May the angels in heaven party hearty tonight. Lord, I pray that You strengthen him in his walk as a Christian and that he may understand and, with Your divine help and the help of the Holy Spirit, ward off all the attacks that the enemy will now wield against him. Lord, I pray Americans will open their eyes and see the threat against them. Lord, empower them to act, and may there be a revival of the Holy Spirit in this nation. May we call upon Your name in joy once more. In Jesus' name and on the blood He shed, we pray, amen!"

"Amen," Thomas added. "Thanks, Sam."

"My pleasure, roomy."

"I'm going to get ready for tonight. I asked Joy Hareld to come with us."

"Who?"

"Joy Hareld, a freshman in my algebra class," Thomas said.

"Oh, yeah," Sam responded. "I know her. She's kind of plain though, isn't she?"

Thomas shrugged, "Well, she's nice though."

"Wow!" Sam said, "The Holy Spirit worked fast on you."

It was just a little after five when Thomas climbed the stairs of the dorm to Joy's floor. What had made him ask her out? She just wasn't his type. Well, it's not like he had asked her to go steady. This was just one date. Who knows? Maybe they could develop a friendship. Men and women could be friends.

He was just friends with Tami and Rebecca. Thomas always thought John was the luckiest of the guys being with Rebecca. She was classy. Thomas figured if he ever settled down, it would be with a girl like Rebecca. Although he considered Dori a friend, he still entertained romantic thoughts about her. She wasn't the type of girl he wanted to settle down with, but he felt a brief fling might be fun. One's worldly self is slow to fade.

As Thomas stood before Joy's door, he said to himself, *At least she is a real nice girl. That counts for something.* He knocked on the door and waited.

After a few seconds the door opened. There before him stood the most beautiful woman Thomas had ever seen. She had styled her brown hair so her feathered bangs framed her face and ended in long, flowing curls. Her full lips were painted pink, and her wide, brown eyes were accented with earthy tones and hints of pink. She wore a form-fitting, soft pink sweater that revealed an hourglass figure and a flat, tight stomach. Her jeans were stylishly form-fitting, and the two-inch heeled sandals helped to shape and lengthen her legs. Thomas felt his heart beating faster and his palms becoming clammy. Why hadn't he met this girl earlier? He finally managed, "My name is Thomas. I've come to pick up Joy."

The woman got a strange look on her face and said, "Of course you have, silly. I'm ready. Let me get my jacket."

She turned and walked to the opposite end of the immaculately clean room. Then it dawned on him. "Joy?" he asked.

Joy smiled as she came back with her jacket. She handed it to him, and he helped her slip it on. He realized he must have looked like an idiot and said, "You look so different without your glasses." *Good recovery*, he thought.

She smiled and said, "I have my contacts in. I usually don't wear them because they dry out and sting my eyes after a couple of hours. You're also probably not used to seeing me dressed up. I normally dress a little grungy. I learned it keeps the wolves away. I made a promise to myself early on that I would only be with a godly, Christian man, one who would want me for who I am on the inside. Besides, I didn't want your friends thinking you got stuck with a dog for the night."

Guilt about his earlier thoughts rushed through his body.

"You're far from being a dog. As a matter of fact, you're the most beautiful woman I have ever met."

Joy reached up and gave him a light kiss on the cheek, then said, "Thomas, you are such a sweet man!" As they left the dorm she paused by the door, waiting for Thomas to open it for her. He held it opened and she waited for him on the other side. She took his arm as they walked along the sidewalk. Thomas realized that he had found his Rebecca. What a day of revelation!

BIBLIOGRAPHY

Daniel, Clifton. *Chronicle of America.* New York: DK
   Publishing, Inc., 1997.

Davis, Peter. *The American Heritage Dictionary of the English
   Language.* New York: Dell Publishing Co. Inc., 1980.

F. E. Compton Company. *Compton's Encyclopedia.* Division
   of Encyclopaedia Britannica, Inc., USA, 1969.

Founding Fathers. The Bill of Rights. See appendix 3.

——. The Constitution of the United States of America.
   See appendix 2.

——. The Declaration of Independence. See appendix 1.

Grussendorf, Kurt A., Michael R. Lawman, and Brian S.
   Ashbaugh. United *States*

History Heritage of Freedom, & America Land I Love.
   Pensacola, FL: A Beka Book, 1994.

GSA Contract Guard Information Manual, Combating
   Terrorism, April 2001 Revision.

Halbrook, Stephen P., Ph.D., J.D. "Registration: The Nazi
   Paradigm." http://www.constitutionalisttnc.tripod.com/
   hitler-leftist/id14.html.

Hall, Verna M. *The Christian History of the Constitution of the United States of America.* San Francisco, CA: Foundation for American Christian Education, 2001.

Hamburger, Kenneth E., PhD, Joseph R. Fischer, PhD, and Steven C. Gravlin, Lt. Col. *Why America is Free.* Washington, DC: The Society of the Cincinnati, 1998.

Holocaust, The\Shoah Page. "Hitler's Euthanasia Initiative." http://www.constitutionalisttnc.tripod.com/hitler-leftist/id16.html.

Holy Bible. New International Version. Grand Rapids, MI: Zondervan Publishing House, 1984.

Home School Legal Defense Association. "Without Probable Cause." 20, no. 4. July/August 2004.

Hulsey, Martin G. Hulsey. "The Implication of Nazi Animal Protection." http://www.constitutionalisttnc.tripod.com/hitler-leftist/id11.html.

Limbaugh, David. *Persecution.* Washington, DC: Regnary Publishing Inc., 2003.

Lively, Scott with Kevin Abrams. *The Pink Swastika: Homosexuality in the Nazi Party.* http://www.constitutionalisttnc.tripod.com/hitler-leftist/id12.html.

Lott, John R. Jr. "The Bias Against Guns." *American Hunter.* March 2004.

McNight, John J. "Gun Control Has Proven Record of Effectiveness." http://www.freerepublic.com/forum/a38d0fd5f403f.htm.

Newcomer, Alphonsa G., Alice E. Andrews, and Howard J. Hall. *Three Centuries of American Poetry and Prose.* Chicago, IL: Scott, Foresman and Company, 1917.

Precious-Life Ministries. "Hitler and Abortion." http://www.constitutionalisttnc.tripod.com/hitler-leftist/id15.html.

Ray, John J., MA, PhD. "Hitler was a Socialist, & Modern Leftism as Recycled Fascism." http://www.constitution-alisttnc.tripod.com/hitler-leftist/id8.html, and id9.

Slater, Rosalie J. *American Dictionary of The English Language, Noah Webster 1828.* San Francisco, CA: The Foundation for American Christian Education, 2002.

Strobel, Lee. *The Case for A Creator.* Grand Rapids, MI: Zondervan, 2004.

Watterson, Bill. *Calvin and Hobbs: The Days are Just Packed.* Kansas City, MO: Universal Press Syndicate, 1993.

APPENDIX 1

THE DECLARATION OF INDEPENDENCE

Note: The following is a transcription.

IN CONGRESS, July 4, 1776.

The unanimous Declaration of the thirteen united States of America, When in the Course of human events, it becomes necessary for one people to dissolve the political bands which have connected them with another, and to assume among the powers of the earth, the separate and equal station to which the Laws of Nature and of Nature's God entitle them, a decent respect to the opinions of mankind requires that they should declare the causes which impel them to the separation.

We hold these truths to be self-evident, that all men are created equal, that they are endowed by their Creator with certain unalienable Rights, that among these are Life, Liberty and the pursuit of Happiness.—That to secure these rights, Governments are instituted among Men, deriving their just powers from the consent of the governed,—That whenever any Form of Government becomes destructive of these ends, it is the Right of the People to alter or to abolish it, and to institute new Government, laying its foundation on such principles and organizing its powers in such form, as to them shall seem most likely to effect their Safety and Happiness. Prudence, indeed, will dictate that Governments long established should not be changed for light and transient causes; and accordingly all experience hath shewn, that mankind are more disposed to suffer, while evils are sufferable, than to right themselves by abolishing the forms to which they are accustomed. But when a long train of abuses and usurpations, pursuing invariably the same Object evinces a design to reduce them under absolute Despotism, it is their right, it is their duty, to throw off such Government, and to provide new Guards for their future security.—Such has been the patient sufferance of these Colonies; and such is now the necessity which constrains them to alter their former Systems of Government. The history of the present King of Great Britain is a history of repeated injuries and usurpations, all having in direct object the establishment of an absolute Tyranny over these States. To prove this, let Facts be submitted to a candid world.

He has refused his Assent to Laws, the most wholesome and necessary for the public good. He has forbidden his Governors to pass Laws of immediate and pressing importance, unless suspended in their operation till his Assent should be obtained; and when so suspended, he has utterly neglected to attend to them. He has refused to pass other Laws for the accommodation of large districts of people, unless those people would relinquish the right of Representation in the Legislature, a right inestimable to them and formidable to tyrants only. He has called together legislative bodies at places unusual, uncomfortable, and distant from the depository of their public Records, for the sole purpose of fatiguing them into compliance with his measures. He has dissolved Representative Houses repeatedly, for opposing with manly firmness his invasions on the rights of the people. He has refused for a long time, after such dissolutions, to cause others to be elected; whereby the Legislative powers, incapable of Annihilation, have returned to the People at large for their exercise; the State remaining in the mean time exposed to all the dangers of invasion from without, and convulsions within. He has endeavoured to prevent the population of these States; for that purpose obstructing the Laws for Naturalization of Foreigners; refusing to pass others to encourage their migrations hither, and raising the conditions of new Appropriations of Lands. He has obstructed the Administration of Justice, by refusing his Assent to Laws for establishing Judiciary powers. He has made Judges dependent on his Will alone, for the tenure of their offices, and the amount and payment of their salaries. He has erected a multitude of New Offices, and sent hither swarms of Officers to harrass our people, and eat out their substance. He has kept among us, in times of peace, Standing Armies without the Consent of our legislatures. He has affected to render the Military independent of and superior to the Civil power. He has combined with others to subject us to a jurisdiction foreign to our constitution, and unacknowledged by our laws; giving his Assent to their Acts of pretended Legislation: For Quartering large bodies of armed troops among us: For protecting them, by a mock Trial, from punishment for any Murders which they should commit on the Inhabitants of these States: For cutting off our Trade with all parts of the world: For imposing Taxes on us without our Consent: For depriving us in many cases, of the benefits of Trial by Jury: For transporting us beyond Seas to be tried for pretended offences: For abolishing the free System of English Laws in a neighbouring Province, establishing therein an Arbitrary government, and enlarging its Boundaries so as to render it at once an example and fit instrument for introducing the same absolute rule into these Colonies: For taking away our Charters, abolishing our most valuable Laws, and altering fundamentally the Forms of our Governments: For suspending our own Legislatures, and declaring themselves invested with power to legislate for us in all cases whatsoever. He has abdicated Government here, by declaring us out of his Protection and waging War against us. He has plundered our seas, ravaged our Coasts, burnt our towns, and destroyed the lives of our people. He is at this time transporting large Armies of foreign Mercenaries to compleat the works of death, desolation and tyranny, already begun with circumstances of Cruelty & perfidy scarcely paralleled in the most barbarous ages, and totally unworthy the Head of a civilized nation. He has constrained our fellow Citizens taken Captive on the high Seas to bear Arms against their Country, to become the executioners of their friends and Brethren, or to fall themselves by their Hands. He has excited domestic insurrections amongst us, and has endeavoured to bring on the inhabitants of our frontiers, the merciless Indian Savages, whose known rule of warfare, is an undistinguished destruction of all ages, sexes and conditions.

In every stage of these Oppressions We have Petitioned for Redress in the most humble terms: Our repeated Petitions have been answered only by repeated injury. A Prince whose character is thus marked by every act which may define a Tyrant, is unfit to be the ruler of a free people.

Nor have We been wanting in attentions to our Brittish brethren. We have warned them from time to time of attempts by their legislature to extend an unwarrantable jurisdiction over us. We have reminded them of the circumstances of our emigration and settlement here. We have appealed to their native justice and magnanimity, and we have conjured them by the ties of our common kindred to disavow these usurpations, which, would inevitably interrupt our connections and correspondence. They too have been deaf to the voice of justice and of consanguinity. We must, therefore, acquiesce in the necessity, which denounces our Separation, and hold them, as we hold the rest of mankind, Enemies in War, in Peace Friends.

We, therefore, the Representatives of the united States of America, in General Congress, Assembled, appealing to the Supreme Judge of the world for the rectitude of our intentions, do, in the Name, and by Authority of the good People of these Colonies, solemnly publish and declare, That these United Colonies are, and of Right ought to be Free and Independent States; that they are Absolved from all Allegiance to the British Crown, and that all political connection between them and the State of Great Britain, is and ought to be totally dissolved; and that as Free and Independent States, they have full Power to levy War, conclude Peace, contract Alliances, establish Commerce, and to do all other Acts and Things which Independent States may of right do. And for the support of this Declaration, with a firm reliance on the protection of divine Providence, we mutually pledge to each other our Lives, our Fortunes and our sacred Honor.

THE CONSTITUTION OF THE UNITED STATES

Note: The following text is a transcription of the Constitution in its original form. Items that are hyperlinked have since been amended or superseded.

WE THE PEOPLE of the United States, in Order to form a more perfect Union, establish Justice, insure domestic Tranquility, provide for the common defense, promote the general Welfare, and secure the Blessings of Liberty to ourselves and our Posterity, do ordain and establish this Constitution for the United States of America.

Article. I.

Section. 1.

All legislative Powers herein granted shall be vested in a Congress of the United States, which shall consist of a Senate and House of Representatives.

Section. 2.

The House of Representatives shall be composed of Members chosen every second Year by the People of the several States, and the Electors in each State shall have the Qualifications requisite for Electors of the most numerous Branch of the State Legislature.

No Person shall be a Representative who shall not have attained to the Age of twenty five Years, and been seven Years a Citizen of the United States, and who shall not, when elected, be an Inhabitant of that State in which he shall be chosen.

Representatives and direct Taxes shall be apportioned among the several States which may be included within this Union, according to their respective Numbers, which shall be determined by adding to the whole Number of free Persons, including those bound to Service for a Term of Years, and excluding Indians not taxed, three fifths of all other Persons. The actual Enumeration shall be made within three Years after the first Meeting of the Congress of the United States, and within every subsequent Term of ten Years, in such Manner as they shall by Law direct. The Number of Representatives shall not exceed one for every thirty Thousand, but each State shall have at Least one Representative; and until such enumeration shall be made, the State of New Hampshire shall be entitled to chuse three, Massachusetts eight, Rhode-Island and Providence Plantations one, Connecticut five, New-York six, New Jersey four, Pennsylvania eight, Delaware one, Maryland six, Virginia ten, North Carolina five, South Carolina five, and Georgia three.

When vacancies happen in the Representation from any State, the Executive Authority thereof shall issue Writs of Election to fill such Vacancies.

The House of Representatives shall chuse their Speaker and other Officers; and shall have the sole Power of Impeachment.

Section. 3.

The Senate of the United States shall be composed of two Senators from each State, <u>chosen by the Legislature</u> thereof for six Years; and each Senator shall have one Vote.

Immediately after they shall be assembled in Consequence of the first Election, they shall be divided as equally as may be into three Classes. The Seats of the Senators of the first Class shall be vacated at the Expiration of the second Year, of the second Class at the Expiration of the fourth Year, and of the third Class at the Expiration of the sixth Year, so that one third may be chosen every second Year; <u>and if Vacancies happen by Resignation, or otherwise, during the Recess of the Legislature of any State, the Executive thereof may make temporary Appointments until the next Meeting of the Legislature, which shall then fill such Vacancies</u>.

No Person shall be a Senator who shall not have attained to the Age of thirty Years, and been nine Years a Citizen of the United States, and who shall not, when elected, be an Inhabitant of that State for which he shall be chosen.

The Vice President of the United States shall be President of the Senate, but shall have no Vote, unless they be equally divided.

The Senate shall chuse their other Officers, and also a President pro tempore, in the Absence of the Vice President, or when he shall exercise the Office of President of the United States.

The Senate shall have the sole Power to try all Impeachments. When sitting for that Purpose, they shall be on Oath or Affirmation. When the President of the United States is tried, the Chief Justice shall preside: And no Person shall be convicted without the Concurrence of two thirds of the Members present.

Judgment in Cases of Impeachment shall not extend further than to removal from Office, and disqualification to hold and enjoy any Office of honor, Trust or Profit under the United States: but the Party convicted shall nevertheless be liable and subject to Indictment, Trial, Judgment and Punishment, according to Law.

Section. 4.

The Times, Places and Manner of holding Elections for Senators and Representatives, shall be prescribed in each State by the Legislature thereof; but the Congress may at any time by Law make or alter such Regulations, except as to the Places of chusing Senators.

The Congress shall assemble at least once in every Year, and such Meeting shall <u>be on the first Monday in December</u>, unless they shall by Law appoint a different Day.

Section. 5.

Each House shall be the Judge of the Elections, Returns and Qualifications of its own Members, and a Majority of each shall constitute a Quorum to do Business; but a smaller Number may adjourn from day to day, and may be authorized to compel the Attendance of absent Members, in such Manner, and under such Penalties as each House may provide.

Each House may determine the Rules of its Proceedings, punish its Members for disorderly Behaviour, and, with the Concurrence of two thirds, expel a Member.

Each House shall keep a Journal of its Proceedings, and from time to time publish the same, excepting such Parts

214

as may in their Judgment require Secrecy; and the Yeas and Nays of the Members of either House on any question shall, at the Desire of one fifth of those Present, be entered on the Journal.

Neither House, during the Session of Congress, shall, without the Consent of the other, adjourn for more than three days, nor to any other Place than that in which the two Houses shall be sitting.

Section. 6.

The Senators and Representatives shall receive a Compensation for their Services, to be ascertained by Law, and paid out of the Treasury of the United States. They shall in all Cases, except Treason, Felony and Breach of the Peace, be privileged from Arrest during their Attendance at the Session of their respective Houses, and in going to and returning from the same; and for any Speech or Debate in either House, they shall not be questioned in any other Place.

No Senator or Representative shall, during the Time for which he was elected, be appointed to any civil Office under the Authority of the United States, which shall have been created, or the Emoluments whereof shall have been encreased during such time; and no Person holding any Office under the United States, shall be a Member of either House during his Continuance in Office.

Section. 7.

All Bills for raising Revenue shall originate in the House of Representatives; but the Senate may propose or concur with Amendments as on other Bills.

Every Bill which shall have passed the House of Representatives and the Senate, shall, before it become a Law, be presented to the President of the United States: If he approve he shall sign it, but if not he shall return it, with his Objections to that House in which it shall have originated, who shall enter the Objections at large on their Journal, and proceed to reconsider it. If after such Reconsideration two thirds of that House shall agree to pass the Bill, it shall be sent, together with the Objections, to the other House, by which it shall likewise be reconsidered, and if approved by two thirds of that House, it shall become a Law. But in all such Cases the Votes of both Houses shall be determined by yeas and Nays, and the Names of the Persons voting for and against the Bill shall be entered on the Journal of each House respectively. If any Bill shall not be returned by the President within ten Days (Sundays excepted) after it shall have been presented to him, the Same shall be a Law, in like Manner as if he had signed it, unless the Congress by their Adjournment prevent its Return, in which Case it shall not be a Law.

Every Order, Resolution, or Vote to which the Concurrence of the Senate and House of Representatives may be necessary (except on a question of Adjournment) shall be presented to the President of the United States; and before the Same shall take Effect, shall be approved by him, or being disapproved by him, shall be repassed by two thirds of the Senate and House of Representatives, according to the Rules and Limitations prescribed in the Case of a Bill.

Section. 8.

The Congress shall have Power To lay and collect Taxes, Duties, Imposts and Excises, to pay the Debts and provide for the common Defence and general Welfare of the United States; but all Duties, Imposts and Excises shall be uniform throughout the United States;

To borrow Money on the credit of the United States;

To regulate Commerce with foreign Nations, and among the several States, and with the Indian Tribes;

To establish an uniform Rule of Naturalization, and uniform Laws on the subject of Bankruptcies throughout the United States;

To coin Money, regulate the Value thereof, and of foreign Coin, and fix the Standard of Weights and Measures;

To provide for the Punishment of counterfeiting the Securities and current Coin of the United States;

To establish Post Offices and post Roads;

To promote the Progress of Science and useful Arts, by securing for limited Times to Authors and Inventors the exclusive Right to their respective Writings and Discoveries;

To constitute Tribunals inferior to the supreme Court;

To define and punish Piracies and Felonies committed on the high Seas, and Offences against the Law of Nations;

To declare War, grant Letters of Marque and Reprisal, and make Rules concerning Captures on Land and Water;

To raise and support Armies, but no Appropriation of Money to that Use shall be for a longer Term than two Years;

To provide and maintain a Navy;

To make Rules for the Government and Regulation of the land and naval Forces;

To provide for calling forth the Militia to execute the Laws of the Union, suppress Insurrections and repel Invasions;

To provide for organizing, arming, and disciplining, the Militia, and for governing such Part of them as may be employed in the Service of the United States, reserving to the States respectively, the Appointment of the Officers, and the Authority of training the Militia according to the discipline prescribed by Congress;

To exercise exclusive Legislation in all Cases whatsoever, over such District (not exceeding ten Miles square) as may, by Cession of particular States, and the Acceptance of Congress, become the Seat of the Government of the United States, and to exercise like Authority over all Places purchased by the Consent of the Legislature of the State in which the Same shall be, for the Erection of Forts, Magazines, Arsenals, dock-Yards, and other needful Buildings;—And

To make all Laws which shall be necessary and proper for carrying into Execution the foregoing Powers, and all other Powers vested by this Constitution in the Government of the United States, or in any Department or Officer thereof.

Section. 9.

The Migration or Importation of such Persons as any of the States now existing shall think proper to admit, shall not be prohibited by the Congress prior to the Year one thousand eight hundred and eight, but a Tax or duty may be imposed on such Importation, not exceeding ten dollars for each Person.

The Privilege of the Writ of Habeas Corpus shall not be suspended, unless when in Cases of Rebellion or Invasion the public Safety may require it.

No Bill of Attainder or ex post facto Law shall be passed.

No Capitation, or other direct, Tax shall be laid, <u>unless in Proportion to the Census or enumeration herein before directed to be taken</u>.

No Tax or Duty shall be laid on Articles exported from any State.

218

No Preference shall be given by any Regulation of Commerce or Revenue to the Ports of one State over those of another; nor shall Vessels bound to, or from, one State, be obliged to enter, clear, or pay Duties in another.

No Money shall be drawn from the Treasury, but in Consequence of Appropriations made by Law; and a regular Statement and Account of the Receipts and Expenditures of all public Money shall be published from time to time.

No Title of Nobility shall be granted by the United States: And no Person holding any Office of Profit or Trust under them, shall, without the Consent of the Congress, accept of any present, Emolument, Office, or Title, of any kind whatever, from any King, Prince, or foreign State.

Section. 10.

No State shall enter into any Treaty, Alliance, or Confederation; grant Letters of Marque and Reprisal; coin Money; emit Bills of Credit; make any Thing but gold and silver Coin a Tender in Payment of Debts; pass any Bill of Attainder, ex post facto Law, or Law impairing the Obligation of Contracts, or grant any Title of Nobility.

No State shall, without the Consent of the Congress, lay any Imposts or Duties on Imports or Exports, except what may be absolutely necessary for executing its inspection Laws: and the net Produce of all Duties and Imposts, laid by any State on Imports or Exports, shall be for the Use of the Treasury of the United States; and all such Laws shall be subject to the Revision and Control of the Congress.

No State shall, without the Consent of Congress, lay any Duty of Tonnage, keep Troops, or Ships of War in time of Peace, enter into any Agreement or Compact with another State, or with a foreign Power, or engage in War, unless actually invaded, or in such imminent Danger as will not admit of delay.

Article. II.

Section. 1.

The executive Power shall be vested in a President of the United States of America. He shall hold his Office during the Term of four Years, and, together with the Vice President, chosen for the same Term, be elected, as follows:

Each State shall appoint, in such Manner as the Legislature thereof may direct, a Number of Electors, equal to the whole Number of Senators and Representatives to which the State may be entitled in the Congress: but no Senator or Representative, or Person holding an Office of Trust or Profit under the United States, shall be appointed an Elector.

The Electors shall meet in their respective States, and vote by Ballot for two Persons, of whom one at least shall not be an Inhabitant of the same State with themselves. And they shall make a List of all the Persons voted for, and of the Number of Votes for each; which List they shall sign and certify, and transmit sealed to the Seat of the Government of the United States, directed to the President of the Senate. The President of the Senate shall, in the Presence of the Senate and House of Representatives, open all the Certificates, and the Votes shall then be counted. The Person having the greatest Number of Votes shall be the President, if such Number be a Majority of the whole Number of Electors appointed; and if there be more than one who have such Majority, and have an equal Number of Votes, then the House of Representatives shall immediately chuse by Ballot one of them for President; and if no Person have a Majority, then from the five highest on the List the said House shall in like

220

Manner chuse the President. But in chusing the President, the Votes shall be taken by States, the Representation from each State having one Vote; A quorum for this purpose shall consist of a Member or Members from two thirds of the States, and a Majority of all the States shall be necessary to a Choice. In every Case, after the Choice of the President, the Person having the greatest Number of Votes of the Electors shall be the Vice President. But if there should remain two or more who have equal Votes, the Senate shall chuse from them by Ballot the Vice President.

The Congress may determine the Time of chusing the Electors, and the Day on which they shall give their Votes; which Day shall be the same throughout the United States.

No Person except a natural born Citizen, or a Citizen of the United States, at the time of the Adoption of this Constitution, shall be eligible to the Office of President; neither shall any Person be eligible to that Office who shall not have attained to the Age of thirty five Years, and been fourteen Years a Resident within the United States.

In Case of the Removal of the President from Office, or of his Death, Resignation, or Inability to discharge the Powers and Duties of the said Office, the Same shall devolve on the Vice President, and the Congress may by Law provide for the Case of Removal, Death, Resignation or Inability, both of the President and Vice President, declaring what Officer shall then act as President, and such Officer shall act accordingly, until the Disability be removed, or a President shall be elected.

The President shall, at stated Times, receive for his Services, a Compensation, which shall neither be increased nor diminished during the Period for which he shall have been elected, and he shall not receive within that Period any other Emolument from the United States, or any of them.

Before he enter on the Execution of his Office, he shall take the following Oath or Affirmation:—"I do solemnly swear (or affirm) that I will faithfully execute the Office of President of the United States, and will to the best of my Ability, preserve, protect and defend the Constitution of the United States."

Section. 2.

The President shall be Commander in Chief of the Army and Navy of the United States, and of the Militia of the several States, when called into the actual Service of the United States; he may require the Opinion, in writing, of the principal Officer in each of the executive Departments, upon any Subject relating to the Duties of their respective Offices, and he shall have Power to grant Reprieves and Pardons for Offences against the United States, except in Cases of Impeachment.

He shall have Power, by and with the Advice and Consent of the Senate, to make Treaties, provided two thirds of the Senators present concur; and he shall nominate, and by and with the Advice and Consent of the Senate, shall appoint Ambassadors, other public Ministers and Consuls, Judges of the supreme Court, and all other Officers of the United States, whose Appointments are not herein otherwise provided for, and which shall be established by Law: but the Congress may by Law vest the Appointment of such inferior Officers, as they think proper, in the President alone, in the Courts of Law, or in the Heads of Departments.

The President shall have Power to fill up all Vacancies that may happen during the Recess of the Senate, by granting Commissions which shall expire at the End of their next Session.

Section. 3.

He shall from time to time give to the Congress Information of the State of the Union, and recommend to their Consideration such Measures as he shall judge necessary and expedient; he may, on extraordinary Occasions, convene both Houses, or either of them, and in Case of Disagreement between them, with Respect to the Time of Adjournment, he may adjourn them to such Time as he shall think proper; he shall receive Ambassadors and other public Ministers; he shall take Care that the Laws be faithfully executed, and shall Commission all the Officers of the United States.

Section. 4.

The President, Vice President and all civil Officers of the United States, shall be removed from Office on Impeachment for, and Conviction of, Treason, Bribery, or other high Crimes and Misdemeanors.

Article. III.

Section. 1.

The judicial Power of the United States shall be vested in one supreme Court, and in such inferior Courts as the Congress may from time to time ordain and establish. The Judges, both of the supreme and inferior Courts, shall hold their Offices during good Behaviour, and shall, at stated Times, receive for their Services a Compensation, which shall not be diminished during their Continuance in Office.

Section. 2.

The judicial Power shall extend to all Cases, in Law and Equity, arising under this Constitution, the Laws of the United States, and Treaties made, or which shall be made, under their Authority;—to all Cases affecting Ambassadors, other public Ministers and Consuls;—to all Cases of admiralty and maritime Jurisdiction;—to Controversies to which the United States shall be a Party;—to Controversies between two or more States;—<u>between a State and Citizens of another State</u>;—between Citizens of different States;—between Citizens of the same State claiming Lands under Grants of different States, and between a State, or the Citizens thereof, and foreign States, Citizens or Subjects.

In all Cases affecting Ambassadors, other public Ministers and Consuls, and those in which a State shall be Party, the supreme Court shall have original Jurisdiction. In all the other Cases before mentioned, the supreme Court shall have appellate Jurisdiction, both as to Law and Fact, with such Exceptions, and under such Regulations as the Congress shall make.

The Trial of all Crimes, except in Cases of Impeachment, shall be by Jury; and such Trial shall be held in the State where the said Crimes shall have been committed; but when not committed within any State, the Trial shall be at such Place or Places as the Congress may by Law have directed.

Section. 3.

Treason against the United States, shall consist only in levying War against them, or in adhering to their Enemies, giving them Aid and Comfort. No Person shall be convicted of Treason unless on the Testimony of two Witnesses to the same overt Act, or on Confession in open Court.

The Congress shall have Power to declare the Punishment of Treason, but no Attainder of Treason shall work Corruption of Blood, or Forfeiture except during the Life of the Person attainted.

Article. IV.

Section. 1.

Full Faith and Credit shall be given in each State to the public Acts, Records, and judicial Proceedings of every other State. And the Congress may by general Laws prescribe the Manner in which such Acts, Records and Proceedings shall be proved, and the Effect thereof.

Section. 2.

The Citizens of each State shall be entitled to all Privileges and Immunities of Citizens in the several States.

A Person charged in any State with Treason, Felony, or other Crime, who shall flee from Justice, and be found in another State, shall on Demand of the executive Authority of the State from which he fled, be delivered up, to be removed to the State having Jurisdiction of the Crime.

No Person held to Service or Labour in one State, under the Laws thereof, escaping into another, shall, in Consequence of any Law or Regulation therein, be discharged from such Service or Labour, but shall be delivered up on Claim of the Party to whom such Service or Labour may be due.

Section. 3.

New States may be admitted by the Congress into this Union; but no new State shall be formed or erected within the Jurisdiction of any other State; nor any State be formed by the Junction of two or more States, or Parts of States, without the Consent of the Legislatures of the States concerned as well as of the Congress.

The Congress shall have Power to dispose of and make all needful Rules and Regulations respecting the Territory or other Property belonging to the United States; and nothing in this Constitution shall be so construed as to Prejudice any Claims of the United States, or of any particular State.

Section. 4.

The United States shall guarantee to every State in this Union a Republican Form of Government, and shall protect each of them against Invasion; and on Application of the Legislature, or of the Executive (when the Legislature cannot be convened), against domestic Violence.

Article. V.

The Congress, whenever two thirds of both Houses shall deem it necessary, shall propose Amendments to this Constitution, or, on the Application of the Legislatures of two thirds of the several States, shall call a Convention for proposing Amendments, which, in either Case, shall be valid to all Intents and Purposes, as Part of this Constitution, when ratified by the Legislatures of three fourths of the several States, or by Conventions in three fourths thereof, as the one or the other Mode of Ratification may be proposed by the Congress; Provided that no Amendment which may be made prior to the Year One thousand eight hundred and eight shall in any Manner affect the first and fourth Clauses in the Ninth Section of the first Article; and that no State, without its Consent, shall be deprived of its equal Suffrage in the Senate.

Article. VI.

All Debts contracted and Engagements entered into, before the Adoption of this Constitution, shall be as valid against the United States under this Constitution, as under the Confederation.

This Constitution, and the Laws of the United States which shall be made in Pursuance thereof; and all Treaties made, or which shall be made, under the Authority of the United States, shall be the supreme Law of the Land; and the Judges in every State shall be bound thereby, any Thing in the Constitution or Laws of any State to the Contrary notwithstanding.

The Senators and Representatives before mentioned, and the Members of the several State Legislatures, and all executive and judicial Officers, both of the United States and of the several States, shall be bound by Oath or Affirmation, to support this Constitution; but no religious Test shall ever be required as a Qualification to any Office or public Trust under the United States.

Article. VII.

The Ratification of the Conventions of nine States, shall be sufficient for the Establishment of this Constitution between the States so ratifying the Same.

The Word, "the," being interlined between the seventh and eighth Lines of the first Page, the Word "Thirty" being partly written on an Erazure in the fifteenth Line of the first Page, The Words "is tried" being interlined between the thirty second and thirty third Lines of the first Page and the Word "the" being interlined between the forty third and forty fourth Lines of the second Page.

Attest William Jackson Secretary

Done in Convention by the Unanimous Consent of the States present the Seventeenth Day of September in the Year of our Lord one thousand seven hundred and Eighty seven and of the Independence of the United States of America the Twelfth In witness whereof We have hereunto subscribed our Names,

G°. Washington
Presidt and deputy from Virginia

* *

AMENDMENTS TO THE CONSTITUTION

The Preamble to The Bill of Rights

CONGRESS OF THE UNITED STATES begun and held at the City of New-York, on Wednesday the fourth of March, one thousand seven hundred and eighty nine.

The Conventions of a number of the States, having at the time of their adopting the Constitution, expressed a desire, in order to prevent misconstruction or abuse of its powers, that further declaratory and restrictive clauses should be added: And as extending the ground of public confidence in the Government, will best ensure the beneficent ends of its institution.

Resolved by the Senate and House of Representatives of the United States of America, in Congress assembled, two thirds of both Houses concurring, that the following Articles be proposed to the Legislatures of the several States, as amendments to the Constitution of the United States, all, or any of which Articles, when ratified by three fourths of the said Legislatures, to be valid to all intents and purposes, as part of the said Constitution; viz.

ARTICLES in addition to, and Amendment of the Constitution of the United States of America, proposed by Congress, and ratified by the Legislatures of the several States, pursuant to the fifth Article of the original Constitution.

The Bill of Rights: A Transcription

Note: The following text is a transcription of the first ten amendments to the Constitution in their original form. These amendments were ratified December 15, 1791, and form what is known as the "Bill of Rights."

Amendment I

Congress shall make no law respecting an establishment of religion, or prohibiting the free exercise thereof; or abridging the freedom of speech, or of the press; or the right of the people peaceably to assemble, and to petition the Government for a redress of grievances.

Amendment II

A well regulated Militia, being necessary to the security of a free State, the right of the people to keep and bear Arms, shall not be infringed.

Amendment III

No Soldier shall, in time of peace be quartered in any house, without the consent of the Owner, nor in time of war, but in a manner to be prescribed by law.

Amendment IV

The right of the people to be secure in their persons, houses, papers, and effects, against unreasonable searches and seizures, shall not be violated, and no Warrants shall issue, but upon probable cause, supported by Oath or affirmation, and particularly describing the place to be searched, and the persons or things to be seized.

Amendment V

No person shall be held to answer for a capital, or otherwise infamous crime, unless on a presentment or indictment of a Grand Jury, except in cases arising in the land or naval forces, or in the Militia, when in actual service in time of War or public danger; nor shall any person be subject for the same offence to be twice put in jeopardy of life or limb; nor shall be compelled in any criminal case to be a witness against himself, nor be deprived of life, liberty, or property, without due process of law; nor shall private property be taken for public use, without just compensation.

Amendment VI

In all criminal prosecutions, the accused shall enjoy the right to a speedy and public trial, by an impartial jury of the State and district wherein the crime shall have been committed, which district shall have been previously ascertained by law, and to be informed of the nature and cause of the accusation; to be confronted with the witnesses against him; to have compulsory process for obtaining witnesses in his favor, and to have the Assistance of Counsel for his defence.

Amendment VII

In Suits at common law, where the value in controversy shall exceed twenty dollars, the right of trial by jury shall be preserved, and no fact tried by a jury, shall be otherwise re-examined in any Court of the United States, than according to the rules of the common law.

Amendment VIII

Excessive bail shall not be required, nor excessive fines imposed, nor cruel and unusual punishments inflicted.

Amendment IX

The enumeration in the Constitution, of certain rights, shall not be construed to deny or disparage others retained by the people.

Amendment X

The powers not delegated to the United States by the Constitution, nor prohibited by it to the States, are reserved to the States respectively, or to the people.

The Constitution: Amendments 11–27

Constitutional Amendments 1–10 make up what is known as The Bill of Rights. Amendments 11–27 are listed below.

Amendment XI

Passed by Congress March 4, 1794. Ratified February 7, 1795.

Note: Article III, section 2, of the Constitution was modified by Amendment 11.

The Judicial power of the United States shall not be construed to extend to any suit in law or equity, commenced or prosecuted against one of the United States by Citizens of another State, or by Citizens or Subjects of any Foreign State.

Amendment XII

Passed by Congress December 9, 1803. Ratified June 15, 1804.

Note: A portion of Article II, section 1 of the Constitution was superseded by Amendment 12.

The Electors shall meet in their respective states and vote by ballot for President and Vice-President, one of whom, at least, shall not be an inhabitant of the same state with themselves; they shall name in their ballots the person voted for as President, and in distinct ballots the person voted for as Vice-President, and they shall make distinct lists of all persons voted for as President, and of all persons voted for as Vice-President, and of the number of votes for each, which lists they shall sign and certify, and transmit sealed to the seat of the government of the United States, directed to the President of the Senate;—the President of the Senate shall, in the presence of the Senate and House of Representatives, open all the certificates and the votes shall then be counted;—The person having the greatest number of votes for President, shall be the President, if such number be a majority of the whole number of Electors appointed; and if no person have such majority, then from the persons having the highest numbers not exceeding three on the list of those voted for as President, the House of Representatives shall choose immediately, by ballot, the President.

But in choosing the President, the votes shall be taken by states, the representation from each state having one vote; a quorum for this purpose shall consist of a member or members from two-thirds of the states, and a majority of all the states shall be necessary to a choice. [And if the House of Representatives shall not choose a President whenever the right of choice shall devolve upon them, before the fourth day of March next following, then the Vice-President shall act as President, as in case of the death or other constitutional disability of the President.—]* The person having the greatest number of votes as Vice-President, shall be the Vice-President, if such number be a majority of the whole number of Electors appointed, and if no person have a majority, then from the two highest numbers on the list, the Senate shall choose the Vice-President; a quorum for the purpose shall consist of two-thirds of the whole number of Senators, and a majority of the whole number shall be necessary to a choice. But no person constitutionally ineligible to the office of President shall be eligible to that of Vice-President of the United States.

Amendment XIII

Passed by Congress January 31, 1865. Ratified December 6, 1865.

Note: A portion of Article IV, section 2, of the Constitution was superseded by Amendment 13.

Section 1.

Neither slavery nor involuntary servitude, except as a punishment for crime whereof the party shall have been duly convicted, shall exist within the United States, or any place subject to their jurisdiction.

234

Section 2.

Congress shall have power to enforce this article by appropriate legislation.

Amendment XIV

Passed by Congress June 13, 1866. Ratified July 9, 1868.
Note: Article I, section 2, of the Constitution was modified by section 2 of Amendment 14.

Section 1.

All persons born or naturalized in the United States, and subject to the jurisdiction thereof, are citizens of the United States and of the State wherein they reside. No State shall make or enforce any law which shall abridge the privileges or immunities of citizens of the United States; nor shall any State deprive any person of life, liberty, or property, without due process of law; nor deny to any person within its jurisdiction the equal protection of the laws.

Section 2.

Representatives shall be apportioned among the several States according to their respective numbers, counting the whole number of persons in each State, excluding Indians not taxed. But when the right to vote at any election for the choice of electors for President and Vice-President of the United States, Representatives in Congress, the Executive and Judicial officers of a State, or the members of the Legislature thereof, is denied to any of the male inhabitants of such State, being twenty-one years of age,* and citizens of the United States, or in any way abridged, except for participation in rebellion, or other crime, the basis of representation therein shall be reduced in the proportion which the number of such male citizens shall bear to the whole number of male citizens twenty-one years of age in such State.

Section 3.

No person shall be a Senator or Representative in Congress, or elector of President and Vice-President, or hold any office, civil or military, under the United States, or under any State, who, having previously taken an oath, as a member of Congress, or as an officer of the United States, or as a member of any State legislature, or as an executive or judicial officer of any State, to support the Constitution of the United States, shall have engaged in insurrection or rebellion against the same, or given aid or comfort to the enemies thereof. But Congress may by a vote of two-thirds of each House, remove such disability.

Section 4.

The validity of the public debt of the United States, authorized by law, including debts incurred for payment of pensions and bounties for services in suppressing insurrection or rebellion, shall not be questioned. But neither the United States nor any State shall assume or pay any debt or obligation incurred in aid of insurrection or rebellion against the United States, or any claim for the loss or emancipation of any slave; but all such debts, obligations and claims shall be held illegal and void.

Section 5.

The Congress shall have the power to enforce, by appropriate legislation, the provisions of this article.

Amendment XV

Passed by Congress February 26, 1869. Ratified February 3, 1870.

Section 1.

The right of citizens of the United States to vote shall not be denied or abridged by the United States or by any State on account of race, color, or previous condition of servitude—

Section 2.

The Congress shall have the power to enforce this article by appropriate legislation.

Amendment XVI

Passed by Congress July 2, 1909. Ratified February 3, 1913.

Note: Article I, section 9, of the Constitution was modified by Amendment 16.

The Congress shall have power to lay and collect taxes on incomes, from whatever source derived, without apportionment among the several States, and without regard to any census or enumeration.

Amendment XVII

Passed by Congress May 13, 1912. Ratified April 8, 1913.

Note: Article I, section 3, of the Constitution was modified by Amendment 17.

The Senate of the United States shall be composed of two Senators from each State, elected by the people thereof, for six years; and each Senator shall have one vote. The electors in each State shall have the qualifications requisite for electors of the most numerous branch of the State legislatures.

When vacancies happen in the representation of any State in the Senate, the executive authority of such State shall issue writs of election to fill such vacancies: *Provided,* That the legislature of any State may empower the executive thereof to make temporary appointments until the people fill the vacancies by election as the legislature may direct.

This amendment shall not be so construed as to affect the election or term of any Senator chosen before it becomes valid as part of the Constitution.

Amendment XVIII

Passed by Congress December 18, 1917. Ratified January 16, 1919. Repealed by Amendment 21.

Section 1.

After one year from the ratification of this article the manufacture, sale, or transportation of intoxicating liquors within, the importation thereof into, or the exportation thereof from the United States and all territory subject to the jurisdiction thereof for beverage purposes is hereby prohibited.

Section 2.

The Congress and the several States shall have concurrent power to enforce this article by appropriate legislation.

Section 3.

This article shall be inoperative unless it shall have been ratified as an amendment to the Constitution by the legislatures of the several States, as provided in the Constitution, within seven years from the date of the submission hereof to the States by the Congress.

Amendment XIX

Passed by Congress June 4, 1919. Ratified August 18, 1920.

The right of citizens of the United States to vote shall not be denied or abridged by the United States or by any State on account of sex.

Congress shall have power to enforce this article by appropriate legislation.

Amendment XX

Passed by Congress March 2, 1932. Ratified January 23, 1933.

Note: Article I, section 4, of the Constitution was modified by section 2 of this amendment. In addition, a portion of Amendment 12 was superseded by section 3.

Section 1.

The terms of the President and the Vice President shall end at noon on the 20th day of January, and the terms of Senators and Representatives at noon on the 3d day of January, of the years in which such terms would have ended if this article had not been ratified; and the terms of their successors shall then begin.

Section 2.

The Congress shall assemble at least once in every year, and such meeting shall begin at noon on the 3d day of January, unless they shall by law appoint a different day.

Section 3.

If, at the time fixed for the beginning of the term of the President, the President elect shall have died, the Vice President elect shall become President. If a President shall not have been chosen before the time fixed for the beginning of his term, or if the President elect shall have failed to qualify, then the Vice President elect shall act as President until a President shall have qualified; and the Congress may by law provide for the case wherein neither a President elect nor a Vice President shall have qualified, declaring who shall then act as President, or the manner in which one who is to act shall be selected, and such person shall act accordingly until a President or Vice President shall have qualified.

Section 4.

The Congress may by law provide for the case of the death of any of the persons from whom the House of Representatives may choose a President whenever the right of choice shall have devolved upon them, and for the case of the death of any of the persons from whom the Senate may choose a Vice President whenever the right of choice shall have devolved upon them.

Section 5.

Sections 1 and 2 shall take effect on the 15th day of October following the ratification of this article.

Section 6.

This article shall be inoperative unless it shall have been ratified as an amendment to the Constitution by the legislatures of three-fourths of the several States within seven years from the date of its submission.

Amendment XXI

Passed by Congress February 20, 1933. Ratified December 5, 1933.

Section 1.

The eighteenth article of amendment to the Constitution of the United States is hereby repealed.

Section 2.

The transportation or importation into any State, Territory, or Possession of the United States for delivery or use therein of intoxicating liquors, in violation of the laws thereof, is hereby prohibited.

Section 3.

This article shall be inoperative unless it shall have been ratified as an amendment to the Constitution by conventions in the several States, as provided in the Constitution, within seven years from the date of the submission hereof to the States by the Congress.

Amendment XXII

Passed by Congress March 21, 1947. Ratified February 27, 1951.

Section 1.

No person shall be elected to the office of the President more than twice, and no person who has held the office of President, or acted as President, for more than two years of a term to which some other person was elected President shall be elected to the office of President more than once. But this Article shall not apply to any person holding the office of President when this Article was proposed by Congress, and shall not prevent any person who may be holding the office of President, or acting as President, during the term within which this Article becomes operative from holding the office of President or acting as President during the remainder of such term.

Section 2.

This article shall be inoperative unless it shall have been ratified as an amendment to the Constitution by the legislatures of three-fourths of the several States within seven years from the date of its submission to the States by the Congress.

Amendment XXIII

Passed by Congress June 16, 1960. Ratified March 29, 1961.

Section 1.

The District constituting the seat of Government of the United States shall appoint in such manner as Congress may direct:

A number of electors of President and Vice President equal to the whole number of Senators and Representatives in Congress to which the District would be entitled if it were a State, but in no event more than the least populous State; they shall be in addition to those appointed by the States, but they shall be considered, for the purposes of the election of President and Vice President, to be electors appointed by a State; and they shall meet in the District and perform such duties as provided by the twelfth article of amendment.

Section 2.

The Congress shall have power to enforce this article by appropriate legislation.

Amendment XXIV

Passed by Congress August 27, 1962. Ratified January 23, 1964.

Section 1.

The right of citizens of the United States to vote in any primary or other election for President or Vice President, for electors for President or Vice President, or for Senator or Representative in Congress, shall not be denied or abridged by the United States or any State by reason of failure to pay poll tax or other tax.

Section 2.

The Congress shall have power to enforce this article by appropriate legislation.

Amendment XXV

Passed by Congress July 6, 1965. Ratified February 10, 1967.

Note: Article II, section 1, of the Constitution was affected by Amendment 25.

Section 1.

In case of the removal of the President from office or of his death or resignation, the Vice President shall become President.

Section 2.

Whenever there is a vacancy in the office of the Vice President, the President shall nominate a Vice President who shall take office upon confirmation by a majority vote of both Houses of Congress.

Section 3.

Whenever the President transmits to the President pro tempore of the Senate and the Speaker of the House of Representatives his written declaration that he is unable to discharge the powers and duties of his office, and until he transmits to them a written declaration to the contrary, such powers and duties shall be discharged by the Vice President as Acting President.

Section 4.

Whenever the Vice President and a majority of either the principal officers of the executive departments or of such other body as Congress may by law provide, transmit to the President pro tempore of the Senate and the Speaker of the House of Representatives their written declaration that the President is unable to discharge the powers and duties of his office, the Vice President shall immediately assume the powers and duties of the office as Acting President.

Thereafter, when the President transmits to the President pro tempore of the Senate and the Speaker of the House of Representatives his written declaration that no inability exists, he shall resume the powers and duties of his office unless the Vice President and a majority of either the principal officers of the executive department or of such other body as Congress may by law provide, transmit within four days to the President pro tempore of the Senate and the Speaker of the House of Representatives their written declaration that the President is unable to discharge the powers and duties of his office. Thereupon Congress shall decide the issue, assembling within forty-eight hours for that purpose if not in session. If the Congress, within twenty-one days after receipt of the latter written declaration, or, if Congress is not in session, within twenty-one days after Congress is required to assemble, determines by two-thirds vote of both Houses that the President is unable to discharge the powers and duties of his office, the Vice President shall continue to discharge the same as Acting President; otherwise, the President shall resume the powers and duties of his office.

Amendment XXVI

Passed by Congress March 23, 1971. Ratified July 1, 1971.

Note: Amendment 14, section 2, of the Constitution was modified by section 1 of Amendment 26.

Section 1.

The right of citizens of the United States, who are eighteen years of age or older, to vote shall not be denied or abridged by the United States or by any State on account of age.

Section 2.

The Congress shall have power to enforce this article by appropriate legislation.

Amendment XXVII

Originally proposed <u>Sept. 25, 1789</u>. Ratified May 7, 1992.
No law, varying the compensation for the services of the Senators and Representatives, shall take effect, until an election of representatives shall have intervened.

To order additional copies of

DARK
SIDE
OF
AMERICA

Have your credit card ready and call:

1-877-421-READ (7323)

or please visit our web site at
www.pleasantword.com

Also available at:
www.amazon.com
and
www.barnesandnoble.com

Printed in the United States
71043LV00002BA/181-183